My Nebula
By Othello Gooden Jr.

To all my brothers and sisters
for their encouragement!

"There is something futile that takes place on the earth: There are righteous people who are treated as if they had acted wickedly, and there are wicked people who are treated as if they had acted righteously. I say that this too is futility. So I recommend rejoicing, because there is nothing better for man under the sun than to eat and drink and rejoice; this should accompany him as he works hard during the days of his life, which the true God gives him under the sun." **(Ecclesiastes 8:14,15)**

Prologue

In the vast expanse of the Lunar Plane, where humanity sought refuge amidst the eternal darkness, a lone figure stood, gazing at the Earth that once seemed so near and yet so far. That figure was I, Othniel James Goodman, a detective from the Lunar Space Station Police Department, but hailing from the humble city of Cincinnati, Ohio.

I recalled the day my life took an unexpected turn. My family and I were part of the first wave of citizens who migrated to the Lunar Plane. I was merely ten at the time, bewildered by the curious sight of Earth hanging in the sky like a beautiful multicolored crystalline ball in the night. It was a fresh start for much of humanity, thanks to the benevolent Mellis Foundation's invitation extended to my family. I have many relatives that are service workers, public servants, both civil (city workers), and legal (judges and lawyers). Every last one of them was invited to be part of the "Raylorian Dream".

The Mellis Foundation recognized the valor displayed by my parents during their service in the Lunar Prime Police Department. Before coming to the Lunar Plane, my father, Josiah, was police commissioner of Cincinnati. That's how he met my mother, Sylvie, who served under him. Impressed by their unwavering commitment to justice, the foundation sought to honor their legacy by appointing my father as the commissioner of the LSPD. And so, he embarked on a journey to protect the lunar inhabitants, bearing the weight of our family's name and a legacy destined to converge with mine as I aimed to follow in his footsteps.

Yet, it was not the path of a commissioner that I chose to tread. From the moment I entered the police force, I knew my destiny lay in unraveling mysteries and seeking out truth. The shadow of my father's footsteps guided me towards the realm of a detective, where clues became my allies and riddles my eternal companions.

As I reminisce about my first assignment at the tender age of nineteen, a shiver ran down my spine. It was a perplexing case that lurked in the heart of the space station, a veil of darkness cloaking its every aspect. From the outside, it appeared to be a simple theft, but my instincts whispered of something far more sinister.

The moon's alluring glow illuminated my path as I dove headfirst into the investigation. Clues led me through a labyrinth of corridors, where lunar dust whispered secrets of the residents that sought solace within the lunar walls. Each discovery fueled my curiosity, unraveling a web of deception that seemed to reach far beyond its Lunarian design.

Time passed like a fleeting comet as I delved deeper into the enigma, tracing the lines that intertwined the stolen object to an intricate network of individuals. Each encounter brought me closer to an answer, yet the puzzle pieces seemed to rearrange themselves effortlessly, leaving me in a perpetual state of wonder.

And now, as I stand here, overlooking the Earth from the Lunar plane, my investigation reaches its crescendo. The truth awaits, tantalizingly close and yet agonizingly elusive. The case beckons me like a distant siren, promising both revelation and resolution. But will I uncover the final truth? Or will it forever remain a secret, echoing softly in the lunar winds?

I take a deep breath, bracing myself for what lies ahead. The lunar landscape stretches out before me, a canvas of endless possibilities and unanswered questions. With determination in my heart and a glint of curiosity in my eyes, I step forward into the unknown, ready to chase shadows and seek the truth that lingers just beyond reach.

And as I embrace the darkness that envelops the Lunar plane, one thing is certain—someone was manipulating events from the shadows under the guise of justice. I wouldn't know how far the rabbit hole went until the day I was sought out by the Mellis Foundation. They called me in for a meeting.

Chapter 1

The air was thick with anticipation as I sat in the dimly lit room, surrounded by my companions. We were an unlikely group, brought together by a shared destiny that none of us fully understood. I glanced around, taking in the faces of those who had become my confidants, my allies, and my mentors.

To my right sat Ivon Immanuel, the enigmatic figure that had extended the invitation that had changed the course of my life. With a thick beard and piercing eyes, he exuded an air of wisdom and mystery that both intrigued and intimidated me. I knew little about him, other than the fact that he was respected and feared in equal measure within the ranks of the organization known as the Time Travelers' Administration (TTA).

Across from me sat Francis Karr, a peculiar individual whose every word was cloaked in elaborate analogies and pop culture references.

His quirky demeanor and offbeat sense of humor provided a welcome respite from the gravity of our situation. Francis possessed a unique talent for making even the most mundane tasks seems like thrilling escapades, and I couldn't help but marvel at his ability to weave entertaining, analogous stories out of thin air.

But it was Zahra Melech who captured my attention the most. Hailing from the vibrant streets of New Delhi, she possessed a quiet elegance that belied her fierce intellect. Zahra was a calculated young woman who seemed to have an uncanny ability to see through the noise and chaos of our world. Her soft-spoken words held a weight and depth that left me spellbound.

It was as if she knew my deepest secrets, my hidden desires. For in this peculiar mix of individuals, I had discovered something unexpected - a secret crush that had blossomed into love at first sight. Zahra's mere presence set my heart racing, and I found myself yearning for every stolen moment, every shared glance.

As the days turned into weeks, we delved deeper into the secrets of the TTA program. General William Raylor Mellis Sr., the enigmatic figurehead of this clandestine operation, had handpicked each one of us for a reason known only to him and his niece, Sigma Mellis, the program's founder. Yet the true brains behind this operation was the General's daughter, Zyra. She had the info on all of us. Our exemplary record was what attracted her attention. The sense of purpose and excitement that coursed through our veins was palpable.

But as with any great mystery, there were questions left unanswered, shadows lurking in the corners of our minds. What was the true purpose of the TTA program? What were the stakes involved, and what sacrifices would be demanded of us? The more we discovered, the more enigmatic and sinister the program seemed.

I could feel the weight of the secret pressing down on me as I stood in the dimly lit office. The walls were adorned with maps, photographs, and newspaper clippings, all pointing to a truth that the world refused to acknowledge. Two years ago in 2021, the Evanston Massacre shook San Diego, California to its core, but I couldn't help but question the official narrative.

The General, a man of unwavering conviction, paced back and forth, his eyes filled with determination and disbelief. He refused to accept the validity of the many death reports claiming that terrorists mercilessly killed the entire Evanston-Pyun family. I, too, found it hard to believe that a family with such deep connections and influence could be wiped out so easily.

As I delved deeper into the case, rumors began to surface. Mainstream news outlets whispered about the Evanstons' alleged tampering with the Global Union of Benevolence (GUB) – a powerful organization that controlled most of Earth's energy resources. It was said that the family had angered the Union with their revolutionary Anti-Gravity technology, jeopardizing their worldwide business interests.

But something didn't add up. The General, a man accustomed to deciphering truth from falsehoods, had his doubts. He believed it was an inside job. Investigative Journalism outlets like OMG and InfoWars echo similar sentiments. The General also believed that there were survivors, hidden in the shadows, waiting for their moment to resurface. And so, our mission was set—to uncover the truth and bring justice to those who had suffered.

Naira Hill-Adega, a name whispered in the darkest corners of the Lunar plane, came up in these reports. In the public, she was the Space Station's Defense Administer. A former African tele-evangelist, the General picked her to be his second because of her ability to unify the people as she did in many African nations in a spiritual sense. As a political leader, her job was more of the same but in a different way. Yet using her spiritual background as a basis in crafting her many policies created an air of respect around her. She had many supporters that championed her high moralistic and heavily enforced laws. Though they were written for the entire Lunarian society to follow, she could only have such laws enforced on the Space Station. Connor and Michelle, along with their families were ones that vocally opposed Naira's policies, calling them "too restrictive". Any other person would've been given the boot for their stance against Naira but the Evanston—Pyun families had immunity just like the Mellis family. So, Naira made it her aim to make life hard for them by hurting them economically with sanctions while trying to uncover some kind of "sin" that the public and the other ruling families on the Station would be against.

That day finally came about a decade ago when Naira exiled Conner and Michelle Evanston, accusing them of secret, illegal backdoor deals that connected them to the villainous GUB. The timing was too coincidental. Weeks before their trial, they found themselves entwined with a powerful organization that could orchestrate a massacre. The General believed it was a setup with evidence falsely planted on Conner to get him and his future wife exiled.

The path ahead was treacherous, filled with danger and uncertainty. But I couldn't resist the allure of solving this mystery. With each step, the pieces of the puzzle fell into place, revealing a web of deceit and betrayal. The more I uncovered, the more I realized that the truth hid in unexpected places.

It all started with Asa's mysterious disappearance. One day, he simply vanished without a trace, leaving behind a trail of unanswered questions and a community in distress. As news spread, whispers and rumors began to circulate, fueling the curiosity of anyone who heard the tale.

Before his disappearance, Naira summoned him, Connor and Michelle. All were college students living in the same dorm in Sector B while attending the Lunar Station University. However, Asa had a child by Michelle named Helen. Naira presented them with an ultimatum. Michelle, torn between her affection for Asa and her growing feelings for Connor, was given a choice. Naira demanded that Michelle marry either Asa or Connor, believing that it would somehow lead to the truth. If she married one, her sentence of banishment would be null and void yet Asa would be forced to move to another dorm.

Michelle hesitated. She couldn't make such a life-altering decision without being with the father of her child. Yet Connor was the breadwinner, making 6 figures and more from his LLC known as Evanston Dynamics, a cyber security startup firm. Naira wanted Michelle to choose wisely but saw the lady refused to do so by her the actions resulting from the lady's immoral Lifestyle.

Unbeknownst to Michelle, Naira maneuvered matters to break up this love triangle. The General firmly believed that it was a deliberate move on Naira's part, a way for her to manipulate the situation and make the decision for Michelle. However, he couldn't prove his theory. It was merely a gut feeling, an intuition that refused to be silenced. What added weight to his suspicions was the knowledge that Asa had been working as a reporter for the renowned O'Keefe Media Group, popularly known as OMG. He had a knack for uncovering corruption and digging up dark secrets that individuals in power desperately tried to conceal. He thought that Asa had stumbled upon a dark secret, a link between Naira and the notorious GUB organization or one of their allies. In the General's mind, it was the most plausible explanation for Asa's disappearance. The Hill-Adega family had a long history of silencing anyone who dared to expose their malevolence, and Asa seemed to fit

the profile of their unfortunate
victims.

But that wasn't the real issue.
According to the Nairan Code, a set
of rules governing all who resided on
the space station, their living
arrangement was strictly forbidden.
Punishment for such an offense?
Exile. It seemed like a severe
consequence for a seemingly
harmless violation, but there was
more to this story than meets the eye.

Days turned into weeks, and the
mystery surrounding Asa's
disappearance continued to haunt the
Space Station. The story became the
talk of it, captivating the imagination
of everyone who heard the story.
People speculated, theories were
crafted, and whispers filled the air,
each one adding a layer of intrigue to
an already baffling puzzle.

As for the General, he refused to
accept that Asa had simply vanished
without a trace. He delved deeper
into his past, searching for any clue
or connection that could shed light
on his sudden disappearance. Then

his former lover, now married to Connor Evanston, along with their entire family, were wiped out due to have "allegedly" pissing off a powerful organization earlier this year. He wanted answers and hoped the newly formed TTA would find them.

Chapter 2

As I sat across from General William Raylor Mellis Sr., his voice filled the dimly lit room, recounting his incredible tale of desperation and hope. He spoke of a time when he was willing to gamble everything, even the boundaries of reality, in pursuit of answers.

It all started when Sigma, his brilliant Quantum Physicist niece, approached him with a radical theory. She claimed that time travel was possible, and she had created a prototype device called the Quantum Chain to prove it. The general was skeptical at first, but Sigma's convincing video demonstrations left him in awe.

In one particular video, Sigma claimed to have changed history in a small but significant way. She claimed to have saved her favorite restaurant, Nana's Pizza Joint, from closing down. The rumors had been swirling for years that its owner, Nana Greene, had shut down the beloved eatery after filing for bankruptcy. Her business took a hit shortly after her cousin, Connor Evanston, and his future wife, Michelle, were exiled from the Lunar plane.

The Hill-Adega family economically blacklisted relatives on both sides of their family, making it hard for any of them to make ends meet. Most of the Evanston-Pyun family left the Lunar plane in protest but the Greene family held out. Nana and her parents were one of the few who didn't buckle under the intense persecution. Nana did much as she could to support herself and take care of her aging parents until one day she couldn't. She became a recluse after filing for bankruptcy last year.

Sigma explained that Nana's business had spiraled into bankruptcy, plunging her into a deep despair. In a heartbreaking twist of fate, Nana took her own life after her parents were denied life saving cancer treatment. But Sigma's intervention altered this tragic outcome. Somehow, she had managed to prevent Nana's restaurant from going under, giving her a chance to build a successful future.

As General Mellis dug deeper into Sigma's work, he realized the profound implications of her discoveries. If time travel was indeed possible, the potential to rewrite history and save lives was unimaginable. The General knew he had to support Sigma's project, no matter the cost. Weeks turned into months as Sigma and her team delved into the complexities of time travel. The General's funds poured into the project, and their efforts intensified.

Finally, the day arrived when Sigma announced her breakthrough. Her theory on time travel was about to become law. Sigma discovered a way to alter history on a larger scale, to right the wrongs and bring about positive change. The possibilities seemed endless, but Sigma's ambitions were tempered by an ethical dilemma. She realized that tampering with the fabric of time came with consequences. Changing one event could unknowingly set off a chain reaction, altering countless lives in unforeseen ways. Sigma was torn between her desire to create a better world and the uncertainty of the far-reaching repercussions.

Zyra, her cousin and the General's daughter, convinced her that the pros far outweighed the cons. Sigma let her cousin lead TTA. The General led a nation that would soon be known as Mankind's Utopia, but his daughter would be the one leading time's law enforcement. Both were equally as important as they were powerful. Sigma, who was affectionately known as Dr. Time herself, just wanted to be recognized as the woman who discovered time travel. Nothing more, nothing less.

It was an honor and recognition of my skills as a detective to be invited into TTA. Little did I know that this assignment would lead me down a path of mystery and intrigue. We were tasked with investigating time anomalies and preventing any disruptions to the space-time continuum. But this mission was unlike any other.

As I delved deeper into the TTA, I discovered that Zyra had curated all the data on each detective. Being a law major at the university gave her a unique perspective on choosing qualified individuals for a job that required a non-perverse sense of justice. Zyra seemed to know more than she let on but her pursuit of true justice set her apart from many studying law. And then I found out about the first TTA group, led by my superior, a detective named Ivon Immanuel.

Ivon was the only survivor of his team after a mission went south a year ago. It was him that approached me with the TTA invite. Unfortunately, I didn't realize until now that my father disappeared on his watch. Rage started to build up. Everything that irked me about what happened on that day. My mother crying, realizing that she was now a widow. Then there was me, angry at life taking my old man away from me. I wanted to blame someone.

That someone was now Ivon. I tuned out Ivon expressing his condolences for my loss. I still grieved the disappearance of my father but completely ignored Ivon when he tried sympathizing with my situation, stating that he lost his fiancée, Z'Rhana Kynnor, on the same mission. This wound had yet to heal, and Ivon's presence only reminded me of the pain.

But something didn't sit well with me. Ivon was the sole survivor, and I couldn't help but feel a pang of anger deep within me. He made my mother a widow, and the weight of that responsibility weighed heavily on my heart. I knew it was irrational, but grief has a way of clouding one's judgment.

I kept my anger to myself, but my words towards Ivon were sharp and rude. It was a release, a venting of the frustration I had been feeling for so long. But as I looked into Ivon's eyes, I could see the guilt and sorrow hidden beneath his tough exterior.

The others in the room sat there in silence as they were taken back by my outburst. Ivon broke the silence, believing my anger against him was well deserved. What?! I don't know about you but something about his explanation and perceived empathy felt disingenuous, all the way down to his apology. Though I said I forgave him, deep down inside, I believed the man was a fraud and a murderer.

Chapter 3

As I stood in the dimly lit room, surrounded by my two fellow companions, Francis and Zahra, a sense of excitement and trepidation filled the air. We were about to embark on our first mission, a journey that would take us back in time to the year 2021, in the bustling city of San Diego, California.

We each possessed a quantum chain replica. These versions were less bulky than Sigma's prototype and were a bit more stylish. Yet Ivon was the only one with a hand bracelet version—but a bit more bling, bling. With these gadgets, we now possessed the ability to traverse through time and alter its course. Our mission was no ordinary one; we were tasked with saving a missing child, Kayleen Evanston, during a horrific terrorist attack that would shake the city to its core.

However, there was an additional twist to our mission. The General wanted us to test the boundaries of time travel, to see if warning the Evanston family about the imminent danger they faced would change the course of history. It was a risk, but one we were willing to take.

Upon activation, the medallions in the center of our necklaces started to glow. A giant luminescent portal, like a circular cut in reality, faded into view before us. As we all stepped through it, the world around us morphed and twisted, and in an instant, we were transported to the night before the dreadful massacre. The air was heavy with excitement as we made our way to the Evanston residence, a floating four-story residential business fusion of a structure—a true marvel of a mansion! This place was called Evanston Manor. Evanston Incorporated's bases of operations were on the first floor. The residential areas on the floors above were reserved for family, friends, and company execs. Being hired as security, Francis and I were stationed in the room directly below Connor and Michelle. Zahra's room was on the far side, directly below Kayleen's room.

The Evanston family welcomed us with open arms, their trust in our mission shining through their eyes. We explained the dangers that awaited them, urging them to take precautions, to stay away from crowded places. They listened intently, their expressions a mixture of disbelief and gratitude. However, the family's patriarch, Conner, didn't believe us fully, thinking his company was untouchable. He then demonstrated the pride and joy of his so-called well-founded reasoning as he activated a forcefield around the building via watch. A blue dome covered an area of a quarter mile around E.I. Conner left it running for a few minutes before turning it off. For the time being, no one else questioned the safety of E.I. and their families living within its walls. Yet my fellow TTA agents knew better to believe such a magnificent defense system was infallible. Something was going to happen to those defenses the next day and we were gonna find out what that something was—no matter the cost!

But just as we began to believe that we had changed the course of events, an eerie silence fell upon the room. Our companion, Ivon, who had been by our side since the beginning, disappeared without a trace. Panic washed over us, our hearts pounding in our chests. We frantically searched the house, the city, but Ivon was nowhere to be found.

With heavy hearts, we realized that altering the timeline had consequences. The very fabric of time seemed to rebel against our interference. Our mission had taken an unexpected turn, becoming a mystery within a mystery. Yet my skepticism lied in Ivon's strange disappearance.

As the sun set on the San Diego's more rural areas, there was a sense of anticipation lingering in the air. The Evanstons, a couple deeply in love, were eagerly preparing to celebrate two important milestones—their first year of marriage and their seventh year E.I.'s existence as a company. The grand celebration was to be held in the majestic Evanston Manor's bottom floor. The place was abuzz with excitement as guests adorned in their finest attire began to arrive, their laughter and merry chatter filling the hallways.

Amidst the sea of well-wishers, I sought out Zahra sitting at a table with Kayleen. Her dark eyes sparkled with a combination of excitement and trepidation as Othniel extended his hand, inviting her to dance. Zahra was reluctant at first because she felt Kayleen needed to be supervised. The seven-year-old girl took offense, believing she was old enough to take care of herself. She insisted that I dance with Zahra, shipping us both as a couple. This notion stunned me. I stuttered in nervousness, trying to refute Kayleen's assumption until Zahra put her soft left hand on my lips and hushed me. She pulled me close and whispered in my ear that Kayleen was quite the observant little girl and knew I liked the female on my team.

Zahra's sweet voice calmed me as she positioned herself in a dancing position, swaying to the slow melodic tunes that filled the ballroom. Both of us began to dance together.

Just as our feet glided across the dance floor, Zahra's gaze flickered, her attention caught by a flash of movement in the dimly lit hallway behind us. A strange figure seemed to materialize for a mere moment before disappearing into thin air. Instinctively, Zahra broke away from my embrace as the figure's presence piqued her curiosity.

Alone in the hauntingly quiet corridor, Zahra followed the phantom presence, her heart pounding. The air grew thick with tension, and she couldn't shake the feeling of being watched. As she turned a corner, she stumbled upon a sight that chilled her to the core. In each generator room, there were hidden explosives, ticking ominously towards destruction.

Time seemed to stand still as panic engulfed her. Zahra's mind raced as she desperately tried nearing the bombs, her hands trembling with fear. But her efforts were in vain as she told the team over coms that the shadowy figure had Raylorian grade robots with them. These bots prevented her from getting any closer. She could only watch in horror as each bomb went off in each generator room. The deafening explosions reverberated through the elegant halls, shattering the serenity of the night.

Chaos ensued as terrorists stormed the manor, ruthlessly disabling the forcefield that protected Evanston Manor and unleashing havoc upon the once joyful celebration. As each generator went off line, so did the antigravity systems. The building rocked and leaned towards the ground, sliding everything to the side, then finally plummeting into the dirt underneath it. Guests scattered, seeking shelter and safety amidst the madness, as everything not secured to the floor slid to the side of the building closest to the ground. The experience felt like we in a ship starting to sink.

Over coms, Zahra's voice quivered with a mix of panic and determination. She claimed that the saboteur looked like Ivon. Her voice laced with disappointment for failing to disarm the bombs. At first I didn't believe her yet my current skepticism of our mentor had me thinking otherwise. Ivon was nowhere in sight yet someone looking like him, according to Zahra, shows up as a party crasher— suspicious!

Though Zahra wanted to pursue them, our first priority was to protecting the Evanston-Pyun family and getting them out the building safely. Zahra took Laina Pyun, Michelle's sister, and Kayleen with her. My focus was on protecting Conner and Michelle while Francis helped with the evacuating other family members. The task seemed easy until the assassins started pursuing us. Francis came in with the rear assist, making our escape a success. In the rubble of Evanston

Manor, body doubles were left to make it look like Connor and Michelle were dead. The death toll kept rising as more futuristic looking robots owned by the GUB bombarded the area with artillery, soon reducing the pride and joy of the Evanston-Pyun family to ruins.

Francis ranted and raved about this rescue gig not being part of our mission but I explained that we couldn't just let the Evanstons die at the hands of GUB. When Zahra rejoined the group, she mentions leading Laina and Kayleen out through the valley behind Evanston Manor through the vineyards. This was the place we all agreed to rendezvous. Though there was something else she wasn't telling me. I reached out to touch her shoulder and she gave way to tears, hugging me tightly. At first I assumed the worst—Both Kayleen and her aunt were killed but she assured me that the two were fine but then I realized time travel had taken a harder toll on her. Zahra began to explain to us all that it took her many tries to get this desired outcome. She was crying tears of joy yet the ordeal of many redos and seeing the two die many times at the hands of the GUB after them was too much. Zahra was at wits end. She wanted to go home.

I never expected this mission to take such a mysterious turn. It was our duty to guide Connor and Michelle to safety. Little did I know, the journey would unravel secrets that sent shivers down my spine. We were traversing through one of the Evanston's many vineyards, fighting GUB robots. Suddenly, they all retreated as if they were being called off. The dense foliage provided cover from prying human eyes but to an AI, no such thing was possible. I led the way based on Connor's directions. Connor and Michelle followed closely behind Zahra and I with Francis in tow, their eyes filled with a mix of fear and determination.

As we neared the heart of the vineyard, Connor froze in his tracks. His face contorted in disbelief and shock. It was as if he had stumbled upon a long-lost secret, hidden in plain sight. His voice trembled as he uttered words that shook us to the core.

"Someone knew how to shut down all the defenses protecting E.I. And planted those bombs. My security staff caught one guy earlier but I see now that it was far too late!" Connor whispered, his voice barely audible. "Who could've planned all this and why?"

We were stumped, our minds racing to comprehend the implications of Connor's revelation. Before we could gather our thoughts, fate intervened in the form of a woman named Val. She appeared out of nowhere, blending seamlessly into the shadows. Val brought with her a tale of urgency and purpose, claiming that she had been sent to meet with our team by the General. She spoke of a safe house, a sanctuary where the Evanstons could find solace amidst the chaos. Her words seemed genuine, convincing us that she was on our side. As we contemplated Val's proposition, she disappeared into thin air through what seemed like a portal similar in appearance to ours. The Evanstons, caught between fear and hope, took a leap of faith and followed her. And just like that, they were gone, leaving us three standing there in bewilderment.

Hours passed as we tried to make sense of what had transpired. Doubt and suspicion crept into our minds, clouding our judgment. Who was Val? Was she truly an ally, or was she working for forces beyond our comprehension?

We went on our way to a nearby hotel, where we were meant to rendezvous with Ivon. All of us were waiting for Ivon to show up. I stayed outside the room, posted by the elevator. His tardiness irritated me much. In the distance, I spotted her—Val, standing at the end of the hallway near our room.

My mind raced with confusion and disbelief as a saw a ghastly figure of Val in the corner of my eye. When I turned towards her, she began to speak. The first thing she told me was that the image I saw of her was a projection—she wasn't really there and couldn't be because of safety reasons. Was this conversation with Val really happening or was my imagination playing tricks on me? The words she spoke, the way her voice resonated in my mind, it all felt so real, yet so unreal at the same time. I couldn't shake off the thought that Val had mentioned something about the future—the evolution of Raylorian technology. Scientists could enhance the human genome. And she claimed to be one of those people who were enhanced. She was someone with the ability to communicate with others through telepathy and could interface with computers. The things Val shortly listed on her superhuman abilities were mind-boggling, to say the least.

But amidst the whirlwind of thoughts, Val had shared something chilling. It was a warning about Ivon. I had my suspicions about him from the beginning. Val urged me not to believe a single word he says, but she didn't elaborate on why or what specifically. The speculation of this unanswered question only fueled my curiosity further, and I yearned to know what Val knew about him.

As I tried to process the gravity of the situation, Val's ethereal image suddenly vanished from the hallway. It was as though she had never been there at all. And just as quickly as she disappeared, Ivon arrived, coming up around the corner from the stairwell. Instead of being angry at Ivon and his absence, I played it off, acting like I was happy to see him.

In the back of my mind, I still couldn't help but wonder: who was Val, really? Why did she warn me about Ivon? What could he possibly be hiding?

The entire journey back to the space station was filled with an eerie silence. The weight of Val's words hung heavy in the air, and I found myself entranced by the enigma surrounding Ivon. I observed his every move, each word he uttered, searching for any hint of deceit.

But the more I observed, the more questions arose. Who could I trust? Was Val the one I should rely on, or was she just a third party with a hidden agenda?

Chapter 4

I stood there, my heart pounding, as Ivon disappeared into the portal. Finally it was time to return to our time and report back to the General. And yet, as I followed Ivon into the unknown, a sense of unease settled over me.

Zahra, always quick on her feet, entered the portal right after me. Her eyes were filled with determination, but I could see the flicker of doubt in her gaze. Francis, always the skeptic, was the last to cross over. He hesitated for a brief moment before taking the plunge.

But when we emerged on the other side, Ivon was nowhere to be found. Panic clawed at my chest as I realized something was terribly wrong. We had all been in this together, planning and strategizing for this very moment. Ivon wouldn't have left us behind without a word. Still, he was gone the whole time while we were in the past. Zahra accused him of being on the enemy's side. At first I doubted that claim until we briefly talked about his mysterious behavior.

Francis shared my suspicions, his brows furrowing in concern. Something didn't add up. We exchanged a silent glance, our unspoken words echoing in the air. Ivon had always been secretive, but this was different. It felt like betrayal.

As we surveyed our surroundings, we realized we were in the midst of a violent civil war. Also, when we arrived was early 2024. All of us believed Ivon deliberately set the date for that year cuz, y'know? Obvious reasons! He must've been plotting something during that time in the past and didn't want us arriving at the time we left. Currently, the Raylorians, as what everyone living on the space station was known as, a faction fighting for their freedom against the oppressive Hill-Adega Family, were engaged in a bloody battle. Her supporters called her Queen Adega. Lives were being lost, families torn apart, and the future of an entire nation hung in the balance.

Naira, the charismatic leader of this insurrection, had secretly planned to betray the General. She called him weak. She believed the people loved her more and had the numbers and support to prove her case. The entire situation felt like a nightmare. Before we left, it seemed like the people were split on supporting her polices and the General let her have free reigns of their government to enforce her Nairan code to the fullest. But have a hostile take over? It didn't seem likely but a lot of those unanswered questions instinctively had me believe Ivon had a part in it.

Al the support Naira garnered of those who believed in her cause had to be from a third party—one Ivon was on. The more we discovered about this war, pieces of this jigsaw puzzle formed a bigger, much clearer picture. There were others, like the Hill-Adega Family, who clung to power with fervent desperation. In the corners of Sector C was an organization known as Project Gene. Their leaders were twin doctors, Eric and Erin Lunningham. Their army was that of genetically modified humans and genetically engineered humanoids. The latter had me believe Val was from their camp but Zahra and Francis, who seemed to know more about Project Gene, said that though the Lunningham's were philanthropists, they would not have access to time travel tech. Sigma's Quantum Chain was proprietary.

What bothered me more was that the Mellis family was not in Sector A. So went searching for them all over the space station. Caught in the crossfire, the three of us had unwittingly stumbled into a war zone in every sector of this place. It was government official vs. Students vs. the Common People—a bloodbath of a free for all! The Queen had supporters in every group. Fear gripped us, but it was overshadowed by our determination to uncover the truth about Ivon. We searched for those clues of where the Mellis Family was hiding amidst the chaos.

We immersed ourselves in the chaos,
searching for answers amidst the
cries of anguish and the clash of
weapons. We became the detectives
in a world torn apart, piecing
together the puzzle of Ivon's
disappearance and the true intentions
behind this war. This was a war of
ideals. Each side had a different view
of justice but those against the
Queen's regime saw this as a fight
for their freedom against her tyranny.

With every step we took, we
unearthed more secrets, unraveled
more lies. The lines between friend
and foe blurred as we discovered the
complex web of alliances and
betrayals that had led us here. And
through it all, we couldn't shake the
feeling that Ivon's vanishing act was
just the tip of the iceberg.

One such alliance was that of Project
Gene. Before the war, their aim was
to improve on the human Genome
through science. However, the
Queen deemed them heretics for
DE'MS behavior. Define DE'MS?
It's short for demonic. Yet this term
applied to all her enemies and we

were called fools for being such. What the people realized that her rule was corrupt to the core. It was found that a truckload of incriminating evidence linked Naira to orchestrating the Evanston Massacre as government agents found GUB affiliates throughout her family. When the General saw this, he ordered she be immediately arrested. Her family moved to protect her and thus the civil war started as more families started fighting each other throughout the space station, trying to either assassinate the Queen or the General. Many believed the fighting would stop if one were killed. The wild card now was time travel. Someone could go back in time to prevent either one's demise or worse yet, erase either leader from existence.

But for now, ensuring the safety of the Mellis Family was a top priority. Now as a front to protect their people, Project Gene allied with a freedom fighter faction known as the Lunar Initiative, led by Alene Lansing. Their numbers were small but help from Project Gene increased their numbers. Alene didn't believe it was enough because the Adegas had more firepower and experience. Then someone on her team had the idea to recruit prisoners within the Raylorian Prison.

It wasn't your average prison. This advanced technologically designed facility housed a giant digital realm. You could tell you were entering a different plane of existence the stepped into the building. The smell of new paint and dry wall filled each cellblock with a heavy metallic smell throughout the entire area. It was a world within a world. Inside, the Lunar Initiative gave the prisoners a choice. Most of them accepted joining the liberation front. Those who didn't were either too sick to fight or didn't desire to join either side. The latter were left alone. Among those who joined were Laura Giordano and Naira Hill-Adega II. I mentioned these two specifically because it was something about them that I felt would change the outcome of this war in our favor.

Laura Giordano's story of how she came to the space station was a dark one. Without going into a lot of detail, the Queen saved her from her mafian family, who happened to be GUB allies. The Queen betrayed Laura's trust when the girl turned to a bad life style instead of helping her adjust to life as a Raylorian. Laura seemed like a natural born leader. At an early age, she learned her family's business and made them tons of money. Sadly, doing so robbed her of a childhood as she experienced many traumatic experiences, including the death of her mother, the famous nomadic evangelists, Marta Van Wundt Schneider, a few years ago.

Naira II, affectionately known as Nai, was in jail just for being rebellious to her parents. She recounted that while other youths were sent to their room for punishment, she spent her days in the juvenile sector of the Raylorian Prison. What she experienced traumatized her and made the girl resent her mother for doing so. After the last rebellious act a few years ago, the Queen left Nai in prison. Nai was filled with an ever-growing hatred for not just her mother, but also her father, Vern, for supporting this abuse. She yearned to see day when both died at the hands of their enemies. Without hesitation, Nai joined the ranks of the Initiative in hopes to not just end the bloodshed but her mother's tyranny as well.

Together, TTA, Project Gene and the Lunar Initiative planned to rebuild this nation but our main priority is still to ensure the safety of its true leaders—the Mellis Family.

<u>Chapter 5</u>

I shifted uncomfortably in my seat, the tension in the air palpable as my TTA team and I huddled around the surveillance screens. It had been months since the civil war had torn our world apart, and our mission was to locate any survivors from the Mellis Family, who were rumored to possess vital information that could change the course of the conflict.

Our hope lay in the Lunar Initiative and Project Gene, both serving as backup as we trekked Hill-Adega controlled areas, searching for clues to the Mellis Family's whereabouts. To our surprise, smaller factions who shared their belief in the Mellis Family's cause began to join our ranks, eager to aid us in our search. And then, just when it seemed like all hope was lost, a crackling chatter emanated from a secret channel within one of these factions. They claimed to be in contact with the Mellis Family, serving as their eyes and ears within the hidden corners of our crumbling society. My heart raced with anticipation as they disclosed the family's hiding place—Sector D of the space station.

Sector D, the smallest and often overlooked section, was known as the industrial heart of the station. It buzzed with activity - relay stations and refineries encircling the station's colossal power source, the Heavy Ion Collider. It was a place where many would dismiss as insignificant, but I knew that the Mellis Family's choice to hide there held a deeper meaning. Automation built this entire space station but the heart of Raylorian Ingenuity began with the HIC. Thanks to the Evanstons, not only did their research create artificial gravity but also making the HIC more of a viable power source than the old fusion power plant down the street from it. The latter still serves as a backup but is rarely used. The HIC was far superior, making fusion as well as nuclear power obsolete.

I couldn't help but feel a sense of excitement mixed with trepidation.

Every step brought us closer to our goal, but it also meant confronting the unknown dangers lurking within Sector D. Soon we arrived at the heart of the sector, where the Heavy Ion Collider stood tall and imposing. It crackled with energy, its hum resonating through the air. The relay stations and refineries, like loyal sentinels, guarded the power source with unwavering dedication.

But as we ventured deeper into the sector, something felt off. The silence was deafening, as if the machinery and activity had vanished into thin air. My heart raced, and I urged my team to proceed with caution. And then, we saw it - a flickering light in the distance. Drawing closer, we discovered a hidden entrance concealed behind a massive control panel. It led us to a secret chamber, where the Mellis Family awaited, their tired eyes filled with hope and desperation. Sigma was there first to greet us. With her were Raylorian grade robotic guardians.

Zyra was with the General. All of us then reported what went on in the past. The General knew we changed it because the bodies of Connor and Michelle Evanston didn't match the DNA samples regularly taken from them by the family's doctor. Yet his voice wasn't that of disappointment. I could hear a hint of relief. He was glad that the Evanstons were saved but he still wondered where they were taken. I mentioned someone named Val.

When he asked me to repeat her name, I figured he knew something about her. Yet my answer was uncertain. She only gave me her first name. The General then filled in the gaps. Her full name was Valencia Valentine and what she told me about her being a TTA agent was true but her being hired by him wasn't. Her story came with spoilers but only what she told him—Val operated alone because in the future, Ivon's betrayal split the organization. Those with him called themselves the United Mercenary Organization of the Terran Elite or UMOTE for short. Val explained to the General that they are responsible for many of Earth's heinous terrorist attacks and assassinations in history. GUB's rise to power was also their doing as the latter was like a United Nations but for every terrorist organization that has ever existed. Those terror cells that seem defeated in the public eye found refuge under the umbrella of their fellow GUB. Within this sanctuary, they became untouchable.

All this seemed too much for me as it was for the others on my team. Zahra though, believed it was a sense of renewed purpose. She reminded me that I've always had a bad feeling about Ivon since learning he was responsible for my father's disappearance. Francis had his own suspicions about the guy, saying that Ivon gave off a really bad vibe when he was in his presence—something otherworldly.

The General began to tell us about the mission that Ivon and his team went on that changed everything. They were to be observers throughout time but Ivon had other plans. Small things the General found out later was Ivon's doing. All of it involved giving Raylorian Tech to ancient civilizations. Some cultures in Africa like the Zulus and South Africans had melee weapons not native to their time period. The Asian cultures had gunpowder earlier than what was publicly reported. Germans had stealth technology and a previously struggling Manhattan Project suddenly was green-lit with a fully operational weapon.

But the biggest and most egregious of them all were the knowledge and power he gave to the Maroons of Jamaica. History says they were never conquered yet the General knew someone was giving them an intellectual push. Sigma's research found that a man that looked like Ivon was with them. Under further inspection, they found it to be him. In the other instances, Ivon hid from the public eye but his ancestry was steep in Jamaican roots as well as Russian and Nigerian. What he did for Russia in the past was unknown but the General had a haunch Ivon and his UMOTE may have staged rebellions leading to a few regime changes within that country.

When Ivon and his team came back to the present from their last recorded mission, only he did. He told the General that an unexplained glitch happened and the two didn't make it. Sigma felt responsible for this happening but later she began to doubt his claim. She has yet to tell that to Ivon's face because he's been avoiding her since that day. He will report to the General or Zyra but if he knows she is gonna be present, he won't show up.

The General continued with his story. In the history books, those who survived fighting against UMOTE in the motherland called him Mwongo. Mwongo meant "a liar" in Swahili. Yet every language spoken in Africa had their own name for him. Upon hearing this, Francis made the analogy that Ivon was a time traveling Judas Iscariot or Devil, perhaps both. With a reputation that African tribes see him as threat to their peace, the connection was well made. But there was more.

Ivon, in addition to being greedy was power hungry. Knowing this, I knew one thing—Ivon had to be stopped. Messing with time this much would have far reaching consequences and a man like this couldn't be left to his own devices. The General mentioned he at first hired Ivon only because he helped fix a glitch in Sigma's Quantum Chain program but he came to her first. This problem in the code stopped the hardware from working. Sigma's finished code led to her proposing the idea of TTA to the General after her father, Norman, loved the idea.

Suddenly, Sigma began to feel extremely hurt by Ivon's betrayal because she opened up to him first, believing he really wanted to help her but now saw he had an ulterior motive. This now called into question his origin. As it checks out, Ivon is Naira's first cousin but canonically, his immediate family hasn't moved to the space station yet—they are still in on Lunar Prime.

Furthermore, Emmanuel is his mother's maiden name but his father is a Hill.

So this Ivon is from the future? Great! So Val's been hunting a rogue TTA agent throughout time. Where does this leave us? Chasing a mad man throughout history? We already have a war on our hands in our time because of his family.

The General believes the only way to stop this war is to get her supporters to turn on her. Doing so was a long shot. It's been seen that her cult will do anything to protect their fearless leader. Yet enough of a shock from something she's done so evil might change that. Francis proposed a better idea. He was joking at first but then I saw the wisdom in his bizarre, pop culture-referencing guru of a detective reasoning. Cause them to destroy themselves and leave the Queen defenseless. But how would we do such a thing?

As for Ivon, we had to leave that fight for another day. Maybe Val

would find some way to stop him. At
the moment, he's not our to priority.

<u>Chapter 6</u>

The night was filled with tension as I made my way through the dimly-lit streets of Sector D, assisting the citizens in various tasks, fortifying the border. All of it were centered around protecting Sector D's only access to the above sectors, a long winding, but spacious hallway leading up to Sector C. It was heavily guarded and the Mellis Family made sure no one got in or out without notice. The air crackled with an unknown energy, a foreboding aura that sent chills down my spine. The sound of distant sirens echoed through the empty alleyway, a clear indication that trouble was brewing in the heart of the sector.

Then dozens of Raylorian grade robots poured into the empty area. Within them, Zahra spotted Ivon. His walked with confidence and commanded his mixed robotic and human army to open fire on us behind the barricade. His tone filled

with extreme malice. Friend and foe
alike were forced to take up arms
against each other, caught in the
crossfire of a battle that seemed
impossible to win.

I found myself alongside Zahra and
Francis, comrades in this
bewildering conflict. We fought
valiantly, but it was clear that victory
was slipping from our grasp. Ivon's
mercenaries outnumbered us, their
ruthlessness unmatched, and it
appeared that UMOTE held the
upper hand. Just when all seemed
lost, a figure emerged from the
shadows and jumped into the fray—
it was Val.

In her eyes burned a passion of
determination. A surge of electricity
seemed to ripple through the air as
she unleashed her powers, a force to
be reckoned with. To my
astonishment, those humans fighting
alongside Ivon suddenly turned
against each other, confusion and
chaos reigning supreme. The AI with
him stop functioning after Val shot a
bolt of lighting from her already
electrically surging body. The first

bolt hit the closest one to her, then chained to the next one until a large group of them started to malfunction and fall to the ground. Those who were far enough away from the danger zone had the sense to keep their distance. They suddenly shifted their gunfire's focus to Val but her image blurred—she dodged every bullet. Cocking her head sideways at them, her eyes glowed and instantly, the squad of bots engaging her exploded, sending shrapnel in every direction.

It was then that Ivon confronted Val, attacking her first in hopes to break her focus. He started accusing her of interfering with his plans, being a thorn in his side. The accusation hung in the air, heavy with the weight of truth. I watched in awe as Val raised her voice, vowing to seek justice for her parents, claiming that Ivon had orchestrated their untimely demise at the hands of UMOTE. Ivon's response was nothing short of mocking, his laughter ringing through the night.

"Justice, my dear Val?" Ivon sneered, his voice dripping with condescension. "You've broken time itself just to sate your thirst for revenge. But no matter how hard you try, you're always one step behind!"

With those words, Ivon's figure vanished into thin air, leaving Val seething with anger and determination, learning that Ivon was never there to begin with. What they all saw was a projection. She turned her gaze towards me, her eyes filled with a mixture of anguish and determination, vowing to find him.

Before Val dashed off, Zahra proposed that she help us stop this civil war. Val was reluctant. At first she didn't want to tell us why but she finally did help I told her that we know about why she came here and it was the General that explained it to us.

"Then you must know that my mission is what got me expelled." Val said with slight agitation. She was looking directly at me when she said it.

Expelled? This I didn't understand. Why? Is not justice served through time travel what TTA is all about? Then I remembered what the General said about how UMOTE infiltrated TTA and whoever the director was actually for UMOTE. After seeing that Val wasn't a sell out, they expelled her. Yet she told me this wasn't the case. Val insinuated that it was something deeper. What was the bigger picture? I wanted answers but concerning myself with events that haven't happened yet is not important, even if the tangent is tempting. Val agreed to help us but in her own way.

After the remaining UMOTE forces were vanquished in Sector D, we moved to the upper levels of the space station to help those still fighting. The situation was bleaker as those against the Hill-Adegas began to lose heart. Learning that the Mellis Family was still alive soon gave them renewed courage.

We made our way to the heavily fortified Holy Manor, the heart of the

Hill-Adegan throne in uptown Sector A. The area was thickly filled with all those in support of this fraud. Seeing groups of them treat Naira like she was a deity made me sick to my stomach. Yet even more sickened by the sight was Val. Her lips were quivering with her fists clenched.

"Can your so-called goddess save you from yourselves?" Val yelled, her voice seemingly booming as if it was the voice of a deity. Her tone was cold, caustic and judgmental.

In that moment, they all turned to look at her and then to us but briefly. They glanced at each other and started to murmur.

"See, she turned on her own daughter instead of being the all loving master you think she is!" Val continued.

The murmuring turned to shouts of hate towards Val. Val expected them not to listen. Then she uttered something obscene as a to cursing them under her breath. A flare of energy cackled around her. Those who looked at Val found themselves paralyzed by her gaze.

With a flick of Val's right hand upturned, she partially opened it up in a form of a cup. She condemned them all to death as she mimicked a heart pumping with her fingers. Suddenly, those before her started clutching their chests and fell to their knees by the dozens. Zahra ordered Val to stop. As much as I wanted to join her in trying to talk Val out of this murderous deed, I felt that Naira's cult deserved this fate. Zahra stepped further towards Val but I held her back. She looked away, horrified at the scene. I pulled her near me into my arms as she cried in horror. My hands shielded her eyes from the horrid scene. The screams of those affected by Val's power raised in number as the victims witnessed those around them dropping dead like flies to an unknown assailant.

Most of them were oblivious to what was going on—the culprit was standing before them! But they couldn't retaliate. What could they

do if they tried? Even the robots
soldiers in with them stood
motionless. They were deactivated
the moment the hearts of their human
comrades started failing. There were
several hundred people within Holy
Manor—of all ages. Every last one
of them suffered from what looked
like a mentally induced heart attack.
They were being slaughtered by the
dozens.

This wasn't right. Many of these
people truly believed in Naira but
slaughtering people just for their
affiliation with a wicked person?
Where is the line drawn?

Suddenly, something broke Val from
her murderous gaze. It seemed to
spoke the girl as if something more
fearsome approached.

"I can't be here anymore!" Val
squealed in fear. She quickly opened
up a portal and scurried through it.

Yet the damage was already done.
As the Raylorians approached Holy
Manor, there were hundreds of dead
or dying Nairan Cult followers

outside in its courtyards. Inside the giant, luxurious mansion reeked of death—there were hundreds more dead at our feet. Death toll seemingly at a thousand, maybe a little more. Those who were foolish enough to continue fighting in their medically weakened state added to the fatalities.

Over coms, the General ordered that the Queen and her husband be found and jailed. To his surprise, they were also among the dead. Many people rejoiced when they saw Naira, Vern, and his brother Roland's lifeless bodies before them. For us, it was a different story. We were there witnessing the indiscriminate mass murder of an entire cult. We were powerless to do anything to stop it! Now thinking about what happened to Val when she first embarked on this mission, I couldn't help but wonder if her sentence was justified against such a monster.

<u>Chapter 7</u>

The General ruled that publicly, the Queen and her supporters were executed. Laura had a grudge against Val but more against TTA as a whole. She had much pride in the Lunar Initiative and to have the win to be stolen by us was unsettling to her. As consolation, we agreed that the public should believe it was the Lunar Initiative that ended them Queen's reign. This satisfied Laura but I could still see her agitation in our presence. Ok I get it! She's a spoiled sport. Good thing Alene wasn't.

TTA should and always will operate in the shadows but for the good of humanity. Our existence will remain hidden from the public eye. I felt the end of this war was near if not already over. But as I learned, this was furthest from the truth. Project Gene helped us up to this point but they became recluse the moment we marched on Holy Manor.

Returning to Project Gene's HQ in sector C. We learned that James and Erin vanished. They were fighting a war in two fronts. Their only help was the Lunar Initiative in helping them escape. To where? No one was talking but Project Gene left behind a legacy of enhanced individuals the public commonly called "aliens". The ones that were the most numerous were the lion-human hybrids known as the Genese. Next were the Nexus, at face value, they looked like regular humans until you took into account their super powered traits—that being their enhanced reflexes and occasional elemental or mental powers.

There were other larger monstrosities not of the latter that ran amok. Many believed the Lunninghams faulted the General for abandoning them to fight those rogue government factions who always had it out to harm Project Gene and the Nairan Cult. As a result, it was found that most of them left the space station in mass before the final battle. Security footage showed that half of them went with Eric and the other half went elsewhere but Erin was nowhere to be found. Where did all of them go? Into deep space I think if not somewhere on Earth or the lunar colonies.

The most chilling of all of this was what the government agents found—evidence of other "test-tube aliens" created by both scientists. Both Eric and Erin had nearly an equal amount of species created under their names. The most puzzling was a single chimera file the Raylorian government found—Erica. Out of all that Erin successfully created, Erica was never released. Or was she? The file only mentioned that it was a calico cat. But there was something that this file didn't explain. What made Erica so special? Why was the file encrypted unlike the files on all the other species? Most importantly, what happened to the project and why it never saw the light of day?

For now, we had to find this secret lab within the compound. It was rumored that the premises had a lot of hidden rooms for solitary experiments within soundproof rooms. Some rooms were found in them dead or dying beings strapped to chairs or tables while others reeked with the putrid odor of decay. My team and I were called to search the Project Gene compound with the help of Laura and Alene. The government helped with the search on the upper levels. We looked for any clue that could lead us to the truth. The further we traveled into the place, I noticed Laura being a bit apprehensive.

Was it fear of the unknown or something else? I would soon find out. We found a stairwell leading to place not yet explored. At the bottom of it was a biometric scanner connected to a large titanium door. I assumed that this biometric scanner only let trusted people in like the Lunningham's or one of their projects. We tried using DNA prints from both doctors but were denied access. Out of frustration, Laura punched the console and unknowingly unlocked the pad. To our surprise, the computer recognized Laura as one of the

Nexus. Wait—what?! How?! I thought she was human!

Laura explained to us that her dealings with Project Gene were what made her a target of the Queen. Out of depression and drowning in her sorrow of not being able to cope with her troubled past, she picked a fight with a humanoid beast known as Avan Sorre shortly after she was brought to the space station. He knew Laura was trying to get him to kill her and he tried many times to talk her out of it but she insisted. When he refused, she attacked him. His feral instincts kicked in and granted her wish. However, just when she fainted from the blood loss, she awakened hours later to be in a new body. Erin transferred Laura's consciousness into the body of a Nexus being created in the image of her old body.

Before the war, Naira knew something was different about Laura. Upon further inspection, her men found she wasn't human anymore. They captured Laura and had her incarcerated. The bad lifestyle the public was told Laura was jailed for was a cover. Naira always had a problem with the Lunninghams and did everything in her power to economically sanction them in efforts to force them off the space station like they did the Evanston's family and their supporters. Exile wasn't possible because the Lunningham's "children" protected them. After the war, the Lunninghams had enough and left on their own volition.

The last remaining mystery led back to Erica. Searching the lab, we found a tall, cylinder like vessel hooked to a deactivated computer. On a panel below it read, "Erica". When Laura touched the computer screen, it lit up. It showed progress bar at 100%. The words "transfer complete".

Francis insisted on finding a body. He believed it would still be hooked up to it. Before we could we heard Erin's voice on the computer. It was a will and testament to her greatest invention, Erica the Calico Cat Chimera. She explained that Erica had the ability to absorb all types of energy and use it to reshape reality. However, the only con that it would age her and make the body more human. She can be functionally immortal through the energy she absorbs but she would lose her car like appearance. She boasted that not even her bother was this smart to come up with a superior chimera as her. The only problem she saw with Erica was her feline traits that would sometimes over power her human intellect. She believes Erica would grow into her human side the more she matured.

The transmission ended and another one started. It was recorded from one of the Nexus with her. They were urging Erin to hurry as the Hill-Adegans were nearing their location. They recount that her brother already left with his "children" to a place called Beta Prime. When the footage got to where Erin was, she was on the table with a bottle of nano-cyanide in her hand on her chest. Suddenly, a Calico cat speaks to them after coming from under the table. Telling them it's her and said the project was a success.

Immediately, one of the Nexus kneels down and lets Erica climb up on them. Several swampy moss-like humanoid creatures join the Nexus. They ask her where should they go.

Erica commands the moss humanoids, she calls the Gridth, through a different portal to the Vortex Galaxy. She jumps onto the shoulders of one of them. Erica apologizes to the Nexus for jumping ship but she believes her powers would flourish more in a place swarming with all types of cosmic radiation than on Beta Prime. Plus she's still mad at her brother for leaving her to fight the Queen all by herself.

One of the Nexus asked Erin if she was still mad about Lunningham using the Zephyran to wipe out her Atlanteans in the past and Erin said she forgot all about that debacle but believes their descendants, known as the Echna'quis of Planet Quang, will have their revenge one day. Their civilization needs to get stronger than their adversaries, which she believes will be very soon. They already have the time travel tech to hunt the Zephyrans. For now they're safe in their home deep within the Andromeda Galaxy. Both the Nexus and the Gridth go through different portals and the transmission cuts before the Nexus holding the camera steps through the portal.

The videos were interesting to say the least. The problem we find is that the Lunningham's left much of Project Gene on the space station, making these monsters our problem when they decide to terrorize the public. Still, better times were ahead. There was a long road before us during this period of reconstruction. The Queen's reign left a bad taste in everyone's mouth and it was found that not all of her supporters were rounded up. The General went to great lengths to expose and trick many of them out of hiding and successfully did. Some chose exile while others chose death. Either way, the space station was finally rid of this cancerous cult.

As the years progressed, the General's health deteriorated. He started having seizures, severe blackouts, and muscle weakness. In the fall of 2025, General William Raylor Mellis Sr. died of a brain tumor. Many of us reflected on the second chance he gave mankind to start over in a society set out to be our utopia. Even though the civil war divided the nation, the Raylorians came together and overcame those odds.

Inside the family soon became a totally different struggle. Many wanted the General's eldest child, Will Jr. to lead the nation but he dean of the space station's university. Will Jr. wanted to focus on education, not politics. Renaming the lunar space station's university was in order and the next leader would have a say so in that. The lot then fell upon the General's youngest boy, Raynard. He vehemently opposed leading because he was a very apolitical person. Furthermore, he was a break-dancer, co-owner of the space station's largest club known as Club de Rayloria, with his wife Jeannine. The club was named after the eldest daughter of the General, Zyra, whose middle name was that.

Zyra took this opportunity to step up into the role of leader of the space station. She already had a law degree and knew much about politics. The changes she made after being sworn in were massive like the cosmetic ones. All mentions of the Lunar space station were replaced with Space Station Zyra or Rayloria. That being said, the Lunar Space Station was now known as Rayloria or Space Station Zyra.

Non-cosmetic changes were as a precaution to any Iscariots in office. If found guilty of treason or any felony, all of a politician's polices were erased from law. With that being said, every policy the Queen ever made, include the ones she made before the insurrection were null and void. Many cheered this day, as the highly restrictive Nairan Code was now defunct. That still didn't stop anyone else from adopting anything from it. TTA was guilty of keeping some of those codes as Zyra believed these specific ones kept morale higher.

Last year in 2024, an unfortunate thing happened when old supporters of the General, who called themselves the Raylorians, started displaying cult like behavior like the Hill-Adegan supporters did. They don't agree with Zyra's policies, nor did they like having Naira II as her defense minister. They despised anyone who was part of that family, regardless if they supported the late queen or not.

This group clashed with the rest of the nation who considered being called Zyrans far superior. Also, the Zyrans supported all of Zyra's policies and defended Naira II against the Raylorian cult mobs. In this uprising, Zyra's stepmother, Anne, was killed. It was at this moment Zyra lost her cool and ordered this cult to be jailed. She loved her stepmother very much and losing her I saw made a part of Zyra die.

My team and I didn't get to known Anne much. We knew that she kept Will and Raynard safe during the war along with the rest of the family who weren't on the front lines. She was a nurse practitioner and knew her job well. The General seldom talked about his family but Zyra did say she had siblings but we never met them. Besides, we were busy working. People in her family said she looked just like her birth mother, Jewel, who died in a car accident when Zyra was a newborn.

When Anne was killed, I felt something ominous brew inside of Zyra. Like she was on the verge of doing something she would never come back from. As if successfully jailing this entire cult wasn't enough. Someone had to pull her away from the abyss. That same murderous look in her eye was the same I saw in Val's. In Zyra's case, she had much more to lose. I learned later that Zyra opened up to Zahra about her fears and her loss. Zyra was able to see that the best punishment for these lunatics was imprisonment and possible reform. Seeing Zahra work not just in this regard but in others made me fall in love with her even more.

Francis and I were out patrolling the streets the other day. He wondered when I was gonna make it official. I eat lunch with Zahra every day but Francis believed I still regarded her as a friend. Hmm… is he that slow? So I had to tell him. Zahra and I have been together for the last several months. Francis acted like he wasn't surprised. Or was he? All he could do was congratulate me on my "score".

Chapter 8

Zyra called my team and I into TTA's HQ fit a meeting. It was a peculiar situation, to say the least. I was expecting another mission but this time was different. I stepped into the area where Zyra and Sigma stood. Suddenly three people came out of the shadows. I thought by their near identical appearances that they were AI clones. Othniel, the alternate version of myself, recounted the events that led him to this point. In his timeline, General Mellis had been assassinated during the space station's civil war in a shuttle explosion and the station erupted in a giant war afterward. But this was where time splintered. In another timeline, separate from both ours, the insurrection didn't happen until the General died of a brain tumor.

Silas and his team first ended up in the first alternate timeline before stumbling upon this one on the way back home. Silas believed that the General could've been poisoned secretly by UMOTE because the timing of his death and the manor of it seemed strange. He believed that In this splinter timeline, no traces of foul play were found in the General's autopsy. There were anomalies in this our General Mellis 'autopsy but the doctors said the findings were nothing conclusive. I was skeptical of anyone saying something was inconclusive. It meant that something was being hidden. The other Othniel believed the General was only assassinated in one timeline. Yet what he saw in ours with the presented evidence painted an entirely different picture. Or am I going too far?

The room crackled with an almost tangible sense of curiosity and intrigue. Listening to their stories made me think about the journey our team would soon embark on. I couldn't help but wonder what it would be like to meet a version of myself that had experienced an entirely different set of circumstances. Both Othniels had different middle names, a subtle but significant difference between us.

The alternate Othniel went by Silas. The other Othniel's middle name was Chris.

As our eyes met, I couldn't help but notice the way his gaze mirrored my own, yet there was something different about him. He carried a bit more baggage as opposed to my athletic build. Him and his Zahra both did. Both Francis 'looked the same except our Francis had a thicker beard while the other kept his trimmed and looked more reserved.

I learned that Silas 'way of approaching things was much different. He was more laid back but still wouldn't hesitate to go at a problem analytically. To my team, I was a bit impulsive. I was very skeptical of new comers, he wasn't. The biggest change was in our family's history. He had a younger sister named Nina. I'm the only child but I do have a younger first cousin named Nina. She has a younger brother named is Othelius. His Nina and Othelius were part of the Initiative, a vigilante group that helped end the queen's reign in his reality. My Nina and Othelius? Both were break-dancers but Othelius was the more famous of the two as he's garnered millions of followers over the years under the moniker, "The Pop'n Lockin' Caesar". Nina was known as the Empress Catalina. Coincidentally, his Nina and Othelius were known as the Empress and the Caesar respectively and were dancers until the rebellion happened. They returned to that life after the war ended. Next difference was Othniel and I's fathers. His was still alive but never joined TTA but was a Lunar Prime police commissioner. Chris never knew his father and was raised by his mother his entire life.

On the subject of Ivon, the one in his timeline was known as Lord Emmanuel. He was much older and has a scar on his face. It wasn't known if Ivon existed in Chris' timeline or not because he didn't ever mention running into him. However, in Chris' timeline, the war wasn't over. The Mellis family was still in hiding.

Silas believed his Ivon was a future version his arch nemesis who probably had a fated clash or several with a much older and more ruthless Val. It sounded like that in one of their battles, she happened to get one good hit in that permanently scarred him. Ivon knew Val was out for blood for having her parents killed but no matter how hard she tried, he was one step ahead of her, always getting away at the last moment. What Silas didn't know was that Val was a rogue TTA agent but only according to UMOTE.

Regarding the differences in our timelines according to the Evanstons, we assumed that in our timeline, Kayleen and her parents were safe. In Silas 'timeline, only Kayleen survived but lived with her sister, Helen, and uncle, Col. Kevin Ravenscraft somewhere in mankind's domain in hiding. In Chris' timeline, the Evanstons had a son named Kaylin and it was found that the Queen had both his parents and Asa killed the day she learned of his existence. Kaylin was also around Helen's age but doesn't have any other siblings. Silas believed his absence from Chris' timeline could've been Val's doing. I began to believe that wherever our Evanstons were in the multiverse, Kaylin would be most likely in the same place or in the area. Not knowing when or where Val came from or currently lived bothered me. The feeling faded when I assured myself that Val wasn't our adversary. That gave me solstice in knowing our mission was successful.

Regarding events in Chris' timeline, they were much more darker. It was a world where the Queen ruled with absolute power. The Mellis family and all their supporters were either dead or in hiding. Chris and his team was the last bastion against her.

Now back to more differences on our team. Both Zahras were practically identical twins. They shared the same physical features, from their dark flowing shoulder length cut hair to their piercing brown eyes, down to the same color red with gold-lined arm cuffs and neck Sari. But their personalities were worlds apart. My

Zahra was compassionate and kind, always putting others before herself. This lady was mostly quiet but in the brain of hers stirred ideas unmatched to anyone I've ever known. In many ways, Zahra was the better detective, calculated in every move she made. Silas' Zahra, however, was more direct, assertive, and unafraid to speak her mind—a bit loud in my opinion. My Zahra was soft spoken. Silas' Zahra seemed a bit unhinged.

As the conversation carried on, it became apparent that the alternate Francis shared Francis sense of humor. We found ourselves laughing at his other self's bizarre jokes, recognizing the strange quirks that only his alternate self possessed. Yet, our Francis seemed to possess an extra wit, a quickness of mind that made him unique.

Silas, was affectionately known as 2kReturner, yet he was the original. Silas really wanted to retire that name. His aim was to take on a shortened version of that identity and simply be known as 2k. I couldn't help but wonder why he wanted to make this change. He reasoned why: Every Othniel he's met, including the one in the splinter timeline, has a codename similar to his. It was too common. Splinter Othniel was known as 2ndMillenium.

He was right. My 2kReturner had always been a gamer tag since high-school when playing various FPS and MOBA games. Our code names in TTA were for fun, not to hide our true identities. In the splinter timeline, Silas said that choosing a code name was mandatory upon joining TTA. In his timeline, it was optional but serious once chosen like a new identity. What was the significance behind our code name as 2kReturner? 2000 AD was the year we were born. As a Returner, it symbolized our unwavering resolve to uncover every hidden truth, even in the face of adversity. Every small point counted towards a larger win if you were to put it in a football perspective.

But it wasn't just about codenames. Silas delved deeper into the intricacies of TTA across every timeline him and his team visited. He mentioned that each one had a tradition of choosing code names as a way to define each member's identities and purpose within the organization. As Silas continued to unravel the tangled web of our existence, I couldn't help but be captivated by his words.

Alternate Zahra, he mentioned, didn't have a code name but if she did, it would match her favorite color, which was Emerald Green. That color matched the face of her Quantum Chain's medallion. But my Zahra chose "Forest Flower" as hers. My Zahra explained that it was a name she adored, a name that resonated with her beauty and grace. I always said she was as beautiful as a forest flower, and she embraced that name with pride. Splinter Zahra was known as Emerald.

Meeting these three was something extraordinary. We owed the safety of the Mellis family to these brave souls from an alternate reality. My curiosity had been piqued, and I couldn't resist delving deeper into their enigmatic tale.

Their Sigma was known as Doctor Chronos. Ours was known as Dr. Time herself. I was told Splinter timeline Sigma was known as Dr. Time or the Time Guru. Regardless of what moniker the legendary Sigma Mellis went by, because of her invention, mankind could rewrite history but more importantly, solve mysteries previously left unknown. On the flip side, with this tech came many woes within a labyrinth of endless worlds, all leading to infinite outcomes and what if scenarios. One thing was for certain: The preservation of the Mellis Family was a must and it seemed that TTA across any timeline made it their aim to protect them. Most of us believed it was mostly UMOTE and their allies that were always willing to threaten our existence.

However, as fate would have it, the journey of our alternate timeline counterparts was not meant to intertwine with ours indefinitely. They believed that in order to truly grow, to embark on a new adventure, they needed to return to their own world once more. And so, they bid us farewell, but left each of us with a sense of longing, a yearning to understand the mysteries of the infinite worlds within the space-time continuum.

The longing in my heart grew stronger with each passing moment, urging me to uncover the secrets that lie buried within the fabric of reality. And so, we set out on a new journey, driven by a thirst for knowledge and a hunger for discovery. With each step taken, I couldn't help but wonder what mysteries awaited us in the future.

Chapter 9

As the sun began to set over the vast expanse of the Atlantic Ocean, my heart raced with anticipation. I couldn't help but feel a sense of excitement mixed with trepidation as my fellow TTA agents, Zahra and Francis, and I made our way to the Canary Islands. Our mission was to investigate a large island that had mysteriously appeared between the Canary Islands and the Madeira Islands. Little did we know that this would be the beginning of an extraordinary journey filled with enigma and wonder.

Zahra and I had always been an inseparable couple, and as we stepped foot on the shores of the Canary Islands, we couldn't help but indulge in the romantic aura that surrounded us. Zahra had a way of finding love and beauty in the most unexpected places, and she believed that this area held a special kind of magic. Francis, on the other hand, seemed to be a party pooper. Zahra and I wanted to take in the sights but he went into business mode the moment we landed. He reminded us not to lose sight of our mission as we ventured out into the unknown. In a joking sort of way, we kinda did lose focus, having too much fun with the touring aspect of these islands.

Refocusing, our first task was to gather information from the locals about the mysterious island that had captured our attention. As we mingled with the residents, we soon discovered that many believed it to be the fabled Atlantis, a lost city shrouded in myth and legend. While the notion intrigued me, I couldn't help but remain skeptical. After all, legends were often born out of imagination and exaggeration.

Zahra began to believe, after all we've experienced, was not to far fetched that someone from the Lunar plane could be behind Atlantis ' arising from the depths. If it was, who? And why? What was their aim? The locals nicknamed Atlantis' WC Island—WC meaning Weather

Changing as the area was known for its sporadic, fast moving weather patterns.

My skepticism turned into intrigue. Suddenly, the locals proposed a daring plan. They offered to ferry us to the island, giving us a chance to unravel Atlantis 'mysteries firsthand. The temptation was too great to resist, and we eagerly accepted their proposition. We would leave in the morning. Until then, we partied with the locals until the late evening hours.

The next morning, as the sun peeked over the horizon, we boarded the rickety boat that would take us to Atlantis. The journey was far from smooth sailing. The waves crashed against the sides of the boat, threatening to overturn it at any moment. The wind howled, carrying with it a sense of foreboding. Yet, we pressed on, driven by an insatiable curiosity that refused to be quelled. Francis got see sick from the extreme tossing and turning of the boat.

As we approached Atlantis, a dense fog engulfed us, obscuring our view of the surroundings. It felt as though we were stepping into another world, one untouched by time and human presence. We set foot on the island with cautious steps, our hearts pounding in our chests.

What we discovered there was beyond anything we could have ever imagined. Towering structures, grand architecture, and remnants of a civilization long forgotten greeted our eyes. It was as if time had stood still, preserving the secrets of the island for centuries.

Francis noticed footprints in the sand. Some were shoe prints while others were the feet of both human and beast. Zahra studied the tracks as we followed closely behind her. She began to see that these beast food prints were not galloping on all fours but in twos. At that moment, all of us thought of one name in connection with this discovery, "Lunningham".

The locals never heard the name before but they were soon going to find out about Rayloria's most elusive but prolific mad scientist twins. We had no reason to believe that any race the Lunningham twins created would be hostile yet we were outsiders. We had to be ready for anything.

As we followed the peculiar footprints on the sandy shores of the island of Atlantis, my heart raced with anticipation. My team, along with the perplexed locals from the Canary Islands that joined us on this adventure, was equally intrigued by these mysterious tracks. They resembled the footprints of a human, yet something else had also trodden on two feet. It was an enigma that refused to be ignored.

Every step we took brought us closer to the truth, or so we thought. The dense fog that shrouded the island seemed to thicken, adding to the suspense of our investigation. Suddenly, out of nowhere, we were ambushed. Before we could react, a group of bizarre beings emerged from the shadows, capturing us without a moment's hesitation.

I could hardly believe my eyes as I examined our captors. They were a fusion of human and sea creature, with fish-like ears, octopus tentacles for chins, and anglerfish heads. Their appearance was utterly bewildering and sent shivers down my spine. They spoke in a language unknown to us, a series of gurgles and clicks that echoed through the eerie dungeon they took us to.

As we descended deeper into the bowels of Atlantis, the air grew colder and the darkness more suffocating. Panic welled up within me, but I remained stoic, determined to uncover the truth behind this cryptic island. The prison cell they threw us into was damp and dimly lit, the walls adorned with ancient writings that we could not comprehend.

Driven by curiosity and a desperate need to find a way out, we pieced together fragments of information left behind by previous captives. Ancient paintings on the walls of our cells showed a portal and a picture of a woman dressed like a scientist in front of it—that lady had to be Erin. The ancient Atlanteans surrounded her. These beings were a variety of humanoid sea creature headed people. They were bowing down to her. In another picture was Erin standing before a giant brain with tentacles. Her hands were raised towards the beast as if like she was embracing it. The next picture showed the Atlanteans bringing gifts and food to this monster.

To our astonishment, it seems that our anglerfish-headed captors were not the true rulers of Atlantis but merely servants of a higher power. A power that remained hidden, its presence felt but never seen. We believed this higher power had to be this fearsome beast. The last picture was a battle between humanoid hair braided plant-looking beings versus the different subspecies of Atlanteans.

The inscriptions below each picture were in an unknown language. Zahra couldn't make out the language of what the Atlanteans spoke to us in either but knew it wasn't alien. Francis grinned while Zahra and I grinned our gears at trying to decipher the writing on the wall. We turned to him after he let out a hysterical laugh. He then told us that these Atlanteans speak Greek. He was tickled by this revelation because this civilization may be just as old as the Greek language, probably around Plato's era. I didn't believe this at first because accounts about Atlantis during that time stated Atlantis was already in ruins for centuries if not millenniums. Francis take on this would seem out in left field but considering the Lunningham's being involved. The war between the Zephyrans and the Atlanteans were erased from the minds of human civilization and recorded as if the ruins were there before the dawn of humankind. Yet evidence was to the contrary. Two alien civilizations were warring in Plato's day!

Yet for now, we had to find a way to escape. Who knows what these Atlanteans have planned for us. What we presumed was that this city was probably hidden in the deep, avoiding Zephyran detection. But why resurface now? What were they planning? With newfound determination, Zahra continued to decipher the writings on the wall that served as captions to these glamorous works of art above them.

Something about these dozens of paintings throughout the area could help us learn more about the Atlanteans. If anything, I felt it would be in our best interest to befriend them. If we couldn't, then it was time to get the heck out of Dodge.

From what Zahra translated with Francis 'help, the paintings spoke of a gateway to another world. It was a portal used by a hand full of Atlanteans to escape the Zephyran wrath during the war. This was technology supplied to them by Erin, whom they referred to as their mother. Some even revered her as a goddess and worshipped her as such.

The common ground here was Erin. How could we get the Atlanteans to

see that Erin was once our ally?
Well, we had to think of a way fast
because the footsteps of our captors
were returning to check on their
prisoners.

Chapter 10

We were led through murky subterranean tunnels towards are destination. The atmosphere became dense and the area hotter as if we were nearing a magma chamber of a nearby volcano. Our captors called the entity we were to be judged by, "The Master Brain". What we expected was to see a similar Atlantean, perhaps a chief elder whom Erin left the care of Atlantis. Then we entered a large chamber surrounded by pools of magma around its edges. Sitting upon a pedestal was a blue whale-sized brain with dozens of squid-like tentacles. Our captors bowed before the humongous creature, referring to it as their Master. The three of us were forced to our knees by being poked in the back of our shins by electric shock inducing weapons.

The beast started emanating an eerie yellow glow as it spoke to us in our minds. My heart raced with both fear and curiosity. The room was dimly lit, with eerie blue lights casting an otherworldly glow on the walls. I exchanged nervous glances with my fellow prisoners, Zahra and Francis, as we listened intently to the creature spoke to us.

Its Greco Roman accent voice echoed in our minds. Revealing that Erin Lunningham created him centuries ago one day while visiting the ancient Greeks. Through him, she created the Atlanteans. This utopia was for all who revered Erin as their mother. Yet this civilization was short-lived as plant humanoid telepaths known as the Zephyrans attacked. Within a matter of a year, the entire Atlantean Empire was reduced to ruins. Previously, their domain was spread across several countries. They had many cities on the outskirts of human civilization but hidden from their view.

These Zephyrans, enemies to the Atlantean people, relentlessly pursued them to the ends of the Earth, aiming to end their existence. The Master Brain, connected to the very core of Atlantis, then learned a vital weakness of the Zephyrans—they couldn't survive underwater. In a bold move, The Master Brain submerged Atlantis, ensuring the safety of all Atlanteans living in the city. Though the city was lost, the Atlanteans emerged victorious. The Zephyrans continuously tried to infiltrate Atlantis down through the centuries but were thwarted by a cyclonic barrier the Master Brain created for its protection.

As The Master Brain revealed these secrets, a shiver ran down my spine. The weight of our history, the power of this being before us, it was all too much to comprehend. Yet even more chilling was its accusation of us being spies.

As I stood before the imposing figure of The Master Brain, its eerie ghastly, cold metallic eyes scanning me with suspicion, I couldn't help but feel a flicker of fear creeping through my veins. The tension in the room was palpable, and every word we uttered seemed to be weighed and scrutinized. Trying to explain our case seemed to only make things worse for me.

Zahra then took over, believing she could do better at soothing this savage beat. She was always the fearless one, approaching cautiously any situation but with boldness. So, she stepped forward with a calm determination in her eyes and began to explain our presence on the island.

Zahra's voice steady but filled with urgency. She mentioned the TTA, and how they sent us to investigate the legendary city of Atlantis. We were not spies, but mere detectives in search of answers. The Lunningham's left Zyra to deep space yet leaving much of Project Gene behind in our galaxy seemed unlike them.

The Master Brain, seemingly unmoved by Zahra's words, paused for a moment before speaking again. Her reaction made him seem more skeptical of our presence. Then she urged him to search our memories if he still doubted her. She knew he had

the ability to search our memories
and find the truth. He did just that.

In a flash, it delved into our minds,
sifting through fragments of our
experiences, emotions, and
intentions. We stood there in silence,
our thoughts laid bare before this
powerful intellect. And then, as if a
switch had been flipped, the Master
Brain's gaze softened. It entrusted us
with something precious, something
that few had ever known. It revealed
its personal name, Cato Gnosis, to
us. It was a moment of true
vulnerability, as Cato placed his trust
in our hands.

Zahra, always so ever caring, smiled
and called him "Cat" for short. It was
a nickname that seemed to resonate
with Cato, for he smiled back at her,
a rare glimmer of warmth in his
mechanical features. From that
moment on, we were no longer
prisoners of the Atlanteans but
trusted allies. We were friends with a
common goal. The Atlanteans
recount that outside Erin, no human
has befriended them beyond some of
the locals—those being the

inhabitants of the Canaries and Madeira islands. They regularly visited the island since it rose from the depths several months ago. Cato wasn't suspicious of them but was a bit weary of our snooping around. Knowing the truth to why we were set him at ease and he welcomed us as his new friends. He soon explained that the weather changing aspect of Atlantis' geological patterns were an illusion to keep out human invaders. Such a deterrent wouldn't keep out the Zephyran.

Cato had a request, a mission for us that would change the course of history. He asked for our help in storming a Zephyran stronghold located in the heart of the United States, a place known as Area 51. It was a daring plan, filled with risks and unknowns, but we knew that we couldn't turn our backs on this opportunity to make a difference.

But why Area 51? Was this not a place rumored to have aliens in captivity or even possessed tech from extraterrestrial worlds? It was rumor to us as not everything on

Earth according to the military were available to us. The Lunar Plane was still its own entity, separate from Earth. With that being said, the only time any of Earth's government agencies collaborated with Rayloria was on issues of interplanetary security. Which hasn't happened yet. I'm sure there will be in the future. TTA worked in secret so any government agency of Earth would not know we were there. What secrets Area 51 actually held would soon be revealed to us in the coming weeks.

Chapter 11

The trip to Area 51 was unlike anything I had ever experienced before. As Cato skillfully demonstrated the full extent of his power by teleporting us near the base, my heart raced with a mix of excitement and apprehension. With Zahra and Francis by my side, we found ourselves standing just a mile away from one of the world's most secretive and heavily guarded locations.

We showed the sentries posted at the base's entrance out badges that identified us as CIA agents. Although we belonged to TTA, Earth should not know we exist. Who's gonna believe the things we tell them anyway? Time Travel is a thing and an organization utilizes it to solve mysteries? Nonsense! So membership to TTA had to be kept a secret for our protection. The soldiers at the gate eyed us cautiously but allowed us to pass after a quick inspection. It seemed our cover story as CIA agents on a mission related to extraterrestrial activity had worked.

Once inside, we were immediately escorted to the commanding officer's office. The tension in the air felt thick with uncertainty as we exchanged glances with each other. The officer, a stern-looking man, listened intently as we explained the purpose of our visit.

"We are here to be briefed on any extraterrestrial activity associated with the emergence of Atlantis," I stated, trying my best to sound confident.

The commanding officer answered us skeptically before grudgingly agreeing to share the information we sought. As he began to speak, I couldn't help but notice a strange sensation in my mind, as if someone was whispering directly to me. It took me a moment to realize that the telepathic chatter was not my own thoughts but a message directed at us.

"You are trespassing," the voice resounded in our minds. "Leave now."

I exchanged a bewildered look with Zahra and Francis, silently acknowledging that they were experiencing the same telepathic intrusion. This was far beyond anything we had anticipated. We were not alone, and there was someone or something present that did not want us here.

We all knew the Zepyhran were indeed here, pulling the strings as shadow puppeteers. If anything, they were controlling key people throughout the base, perhaps the commanding officer himself. He wasn't forthcoming with all the info he had on their progress, like he was holding back something important.

As we pressed the commanding officer for more information, it became evident that he was genuinely unaware of any extraterrestrial activity or the emergence of Atlantis. It was becoming increasingly clear that we had stumbled upon a secret within a secret, a hidden reality even the military was unaware of—the Zephyran had infiltrated Area 51 but not one person knew they existed.

Cato informed us how powerful they were but he assured us that they wouldn't be able to harm us as long as he was alive. Evidence of this was us hearing Cato's voice in our minds, letting us know that the Zephyrans were onto us the moment we stepped into the commanding officer's office.

With our minds racing and our determination heightened, Zahra, Francis, and I knew we had to uncover the truth. We discreetly began our own investigation, exploring the facility's corridors and digging deeper into classified files.

But the more we uncovered, the more dangerous it became. The whispers in our minds grew louder, more insistent, warning us to retreat. It was as if we were treading on forbidden grounds, unraveling a forbidden mystery.

In the heart of the base, Zahra's gaze shifted uneasily, her eyes darting across the area. She noticed bends in the atmosphere, ripples that seemed out of place. A sense of foreboding washed over us, as if an invisible threat lurked in the shadows. Zahra's discovery was both exhilarating and unsettling. We knew we had stumbled upon something significant, something beyond our comprehension.

Without hesitation, Zahra relayed her findings to Cato, who was still connected to all of our minds telepathically. In response to Zahra's revelation, Cato bestowed upon us an even greater portion of his power, infusing us with newfound heighten senses, revealing things to us previously unseen to human eyes. We were ready to uncover the hidden treasures that were before us.

As we ventured further into the base, our senses heightened, sharpened by the presence of an imminent danger. What we now saw was that the Zephyran had overrun the base. Cato told us these creatures were capable of manipulating minds and bending reality on a small scale. They wiped out most of the Atlanteans. Left unchecked, they would be a grave threat to humanity also. They had to be stopped.

Suddenly, the Zephyran became aware of our presence. They swarmed around us, a relentless wave of darkness, eager to extinguish the light of our existence. Desperate to protect themselves, some of them used the human soldiers as meat shields, sacrificing them in a bid to shield their own frailty. But we knew that our true adversaries were the controllers, the ones who held the strings of this diabolical puppetry.

With every ounce of strength granted by Cato's power, we fought back, our fusion of futuristic a psionic weapons clashing against their malevolent energy based psionic attacks and physical weapons. Without Cato's enhancements, we stood no chance of survival.

Zahra's eyes blazed with determination—her focus unwavering. Francis, with his unwavering loyalty, struck fear into the hearts of our enemies. And I, Othniel, felt an indescribable force surge through my veins, propelling me forward.

Through the chaos, we hunted down the enemy controllers, their presence throughout the base wasn't hidden anymore and Cato knew exactly which ones to target. As we vanquished them, their hold on the once mind-controlled soldiers was shattered. These soldiers, freed from their oppressive control, fought alongside us, their loyalty now to humanity rather than the Zephyran.

The battle raged on, the adrenaline coursing through our veins. But within the chaos, a singular thought consumed my mind—what had brought the Zephyran to this base? The answer remained elusive. The mystery deepened, leaving us yearning for resolution. As the battle reached its climax, I felt a strange mixture of triumph and frustration.

We had prevailed, but the mysteries that had ignited our curiosity still lingered, teasing us with their enigmatic nature.

As the battle ended, we gathered our wounded and buried the dead. These brave men and women helped us expel an extraterrestrial threat and would be remember as heroes for saving the world from it. Yet among us three, somehow we got separated during the battle, Zahra answered on her com and I met her at the commanding officer's office. Francis didn't answer. We called him several times.

That's when Cato revealed to us that in Zephyran's retreat, they took Francis as a hostage. Cato then called us back to Atlantis because of a new alarming development. After saying our goodbyes to the brave men and women that helped us free Area 51 from the Zephyran, we were teleported back to Atlantis.

Chapter 12

The air felt heavy, as if the island itself was holding its breath, an eerie silence enveloping every corner. Something is amiss, and I couldn't help but feel a knot of curiosity forming in my stomach. Zahra walked beside me. She, too, senses the unusual stillness that blankets the island. Little did we know that our return would be met with such a puzzling situation.

As we traverse the deserted streets, our eyes widen with disbelief. The once vibrant and lively city is now desolate, its buildings eerily silent and devoid of life. It is then that we catch sight of the Zephyran, locked in combat with the Atlanteans. Upon seeing us, the Atlanteans tell us that we are needed in Cato's chamber.

With cautious steps, we made our way towards Cato's chamber, hoping to find answers amidst the chaos. The air crackles with tension as we push open the chamber doors, revealing the enigmatic figure standing before us.

"Cato," I breathe, relief washing over me at the sight of his familiar face. "What has happened here?"

Cato's ghastly floating energy eyes hold a mix of weariness and determination as he begins to explain.

He told us he was unable to teleport Zahra and I directly before him because his power was spread too thin beyond protecting Atlantis from the Zephyran invaders. He had to drop the forcefield just to let us in. When he did, the Zephyran got in also.

He implored us to join him in his mission to stop the Zephyran, their dark intentions threatening to consume the island, as he knows they are trying to destroy the Atlantis and himself once and for all. Zahra and I comprehended the gravity of the situation fully. We both nod in to him agreement. We know that the fate of Atlantis rests on our shoulders, and we cannot back down from this challenge.

As we fought with our Atlantean allies m, our path converges with Ivon, a former ally who has now succumbed to the Zephyran influence. Yet I doubted he was ever on our side to begin with. Ivon's half-baked backstory, disappearance on our first mission, and AWOL status during the civil war—It made me say only one thing to him…

"Traitor". My tone was angered and cold.

"You're fighting a losing battle, Oth!" He taunted. His words laced with venom. "Oh, but let's even the playing field, shall we?"

From the darkness behind him emerged Francis. Zahra tried calling out to him but he didn't respond. Then she knew that he was under the Zephyran's mind control.

Adrenaline courses through my veins as I engage in a fierce battle against

Ivon and Francis. I focused Ivon, as I was full or rage and determination to end him. Before I could, Francis jumped in the way, fighting in Ivon's place. I didn't want to fight Francis so I held back. Francis, on the other hand, didn't. His strikes were with malice.

Cato's powers, bestowed upon me, had given me an edge, but the fury in Ivon's eyes is undeniably intense. Francis, trapped in his mind-controlled state, struggles to unleash the full potential of the power Cato granted him.

In a moment of chaos, the Zephyran release their hold on Francis as Zahra enters the fray with a well-placed energy blast, knocking Francis into a wall. He fell to the ground but found to be in a comatose on the ground.

Ivon, disgusted at how the mind controlled Francis couldn't step to us, retreated. Cato urged us to chase him. In the meantime, he was going to send out an S.O.S., hoping that mother would hear him. I was skeptic, knowing Erin was a galaxy away. Cato on the other hand, assured us that Erin has a way of knowing the wellbeing of all her children. How? That remained to be seen. Zahra stayed behind to look after Francis in his unconscious state while I ran after Ivon.

I raced through the winding underground caverns, my heart pounding in my chest. The sound of clashing swords, rapid gunfire and cries of battle filled the air as my fellow Atlantean allies fought valiantly against the villainous Zephyran. Our mission was clear— find Ivon and end him. I could no longer let this piece of treacherous filth exist any longer.

As I dodged a spray of fireballs, I couldn't help but wonder why Ivon had turned his back on mankind. What had driven him to betray his comrades and aid the very enemy we all sought to defeat? Determination fueled my steps as I pushed forward, the thought of confronting Ivon weighing heavily on my mind.

Finally, I reached a small chamber nestled deep within the caverns. There, standing alone, was Ivon himself. His eyes, once filled with warmth and camaraderie, now held a coldness that sent shivers down my spine. I mustered my courage and demanded an explanation.

"Why, Ivon?" I asked as my voice filled with frustration and confusion. "Why did you betray us?"

Ivon turned to face me, his expression unreadable. "Eric Lunningham," he replied, his voice laced with bitterness. "He offered me something the TTA couldn't."

My heart sank. Eric Lunningham, out of all the people? The mad doctor himself had enough power and influence to be unmatched, but I never suspected he could sway someone as loyal as Ivon. Then again, had he ever been? He was the reason why my father and Z'Rhana are still missing.

"What could he offer you that was worth turning your back on mankind?" I pressed, desperate to understand.

Ivon's gaze pierced through me, his voice carrying a weight of foreboding. "Othniel, you must understand. I am not from your future. I come from a future where neither the Evanstons nor their allies are alive."

His words hung in the air, a chilling revelation. Ivon's origins were shrouded in mystery, but his knowledge of a future where the Evanstons were absent was unsettling. Then I knew he had to be from Chris' timeline, not Silas'.

"And the Zephyran?" I asked, my voice barely a whisper. "Do they truly control Earth?"
Ivon nodded grimly. "Through Area 51, they hold dominion over our world. The power they possess is unlike anything you can imagine."

As the weight of his words settled upon me, a sense of urgency consumed my being. The battle against the Zephyran was not simply a fight for survival, but an effort to prevent a future that had been tainted by darkness and despair. Yet one question remained.

"What really happened to my father?" I asked him. That had burned in my mind, itching to be answered. I wouldn't rest till I found out what happened to my dad.

"Back then I was a different person." Ivon said. "I purposely kept your reality's Ivon and his family from ever coming to the space station but I can only prolong the inevitable for so long."

It felt like he was stalling, trying to sell me his stupid sob story of self-pity. I wasn't buying it. I repeated myself, angrier than the first time, screaming at him. That's when he told me.

"Time travel is an uncaring mister." Ivon said coldy. "Do too much for personal gain and your punishment will be divine."

With that being said, Ivon revealed to me that his entire team was lost to time itself. He believed it was divine punishment for trying to change history nefariously. Before Ivon met Eric, he was trying to do fix pre-colonial Africa, in making it a world power. After believing he was successful, Ivon returned to the present only to find matters were made worse. Furthermore, only he returned to the present. Josiah and Z'Rhana were nowhere to be found. Ivon believed some cosmic force condemned in some shape or form. He didn't bother looking for his old comrades. As penance, the General had him personally train the next TTA group, which was us.

I stood there in silence. My mind was at a crossroads. The heart told me to take my revenge but the mind told me what Ivon tried to do was noble. But another part of me took in account his misdeeds. He was allied with a mad scientist hellbent on multiversal domination. Ivon couldn't see that he was just a pawn.

"What makes you think you aren't expendable to him?" I questioned Ivon's loyalty.

"Cuz I knew how it ended!" Ivon sneered.

Knew how it ended? Those words confused me much. Then he clarified after seeing my look of bewilderment.

"Eric became no one in my reality and was deeply depressed after learning that our reality's Naira had his sister and all her children killed. I changed the past to prevent such a future by making this reality's Eric a survivor! In doing so, I made his sister one too!"

Now everything Ivon did made sense. Yet I couldn't excuse the fact that in the process, innocent people died. According to Ivon, his team was still alive but lost somewhere in time. My murderous rage subsided. I couldn't kill Ivon. Though he was an evil little crapper, still the fact remained that he was an enemy of TTA and a threat to many.

"Why aid this sibling rivalry then?" Another question arose—one that bugged me currently. This fight between two of the smartest scientists in our reality had gone far enough. It had to stop.

"Eric wants to be the Allfather of all alien races, including to those whom his sister created." Ivon answered. "Those who stand in our way will join the dead."

Suddenly, I felt this renewed sense of purpose. With it came a rage against not just one man but an entire culture—a genocidal elitist one. Ivon stood in the midst of one that believed one man's ideals reigned supreme. On the other side was his sister. She desired nothing of the sort. From what we knew about her, Erin was a humble human being. If she was nice enough to give Laura a new body, what would she do on a grander scale to one of her own.

TTA didn't know much about Eric but from what I learned from Ivon, the mad doctor seemed to be the real threat to our reality. Ivon was enemy number 2.

"Not in *my* nebula!" I growled valiantly. My voice boomed throughout the spacious chasm as a prepared myself to fight Ivon. I wasn't going to let the Atlanteans or any of Erin's children be killed.

Just as I readied myself for a fight, Ivon shook his head. He told me he lives to fight another day. All of the sudden Ivon teleported out. A short while later, I learned that the Zephyran were pulling away from the island. I returned to Cato's chamber to hear the details.

Chapter 13

I never expected to find myself in such a bizarre situation, but life has a funny way of throwing us into the wildest of encounters. As I returned to Cato's chambers, I noticed him talking to the image of a humanoid cat lady. It was Erin. She was indeed in the body of her chimeran project named Erica. Still, I didn't know if I should refer to her as such or as we always knew her.

I took a moment and gazed at her figure. Erin was dressed in black pants and a blue silky shirt. Her skin resembled that of a calico's fur but was actually that of a human's. The dominant color of it was white but with brown stripes. She had a brown color patch around her right eye. Her short shoulder length hair was blue with half of it combed to one side covering her left eye. She took a moment to gracefully lick her human fingernails as cat claws quickly extended from them. The lady combed her hair a few times as she spoke to Zahra and I as she was asked what should we call her.

"Whichever you prefer!" Her calm British voice was soothing. It was in stark contrast to her brother whom was always seen as a rude and pompous individual.

My mind raced with questions, confusion, and an intense desire to understand what was happening. However, before I could voice my astonishment, the atmosphere shifted.

Erin brought me up to date on her presence when I returned from confronting Ivon. The Zephyrans heard whispers through the subspace chatter, murmurs of a formidable presence known as "the DAD" breaching our solar system. My expression turned grave as I revealed that the DAD was, in fact, her flagship. The Diamond Arc Destroyer, a vessel equipped with impenetrable armor capable of withstanding any assault.

My curiosity piqued, I listened intently as Erin shared her story. She and her crew had been traversing the vast cosmos when she received Cato's distress call. Without hesitation, she rushed to aid her child, only to encounter with her brother and his crew aboard his Lainhardt Omega. Between the Milky Way and Andromeda Galaxies, both vessels did battle. At first, the two juggernauts engaged in a fierce battle, but Eric soon realized the futility of his efforts against his sister's ship. He may have out gunned her but the DAD had superior armor. No weapon in his arsenal could dent the DAD's hull made completely out of a diamond mineral like metallic alloy. Yet her weapons couldn't scratch his urelite alloy hull either—Both were at a stalemate.

However, the DAD was faster than Lainhardt Omega. She also boasted that her ship could run circles around her brother's pride and joy effortlessly. Shape wise, Lainhardt Omega was a battleship shaped vessel bigger than Rayloria. The DAD was a bit smaller than Lainhardt Omega and built in the image of a wolf spider. It's 8 legs were in fact its massive laser cannons but could be used as engines also. Additionally, there were extra engines within the hull that gave the DAD that extra "kick" during travel.

Erin's seemingly more ruthless and strategic tactics scared her brother into running away as he learned that Erica's personality was more motherly than Erin's. This was noted, as Erin never embraced the roll as a mother, until she spent a lot of time with the Gridth, and traveling with them and the Nexus aboard the DAD, not just throughout the cosmos but through time itself. Erin saw it as her growth to a level she believed her brother would never reach. Erin boasts this being the perk of being the older twin yet Eric will lie and say that he actually is. When asked if she believed if she was either Erin or Erica, the lady vehemently but jokingly replied, "Both!"

As the reality of their encounter sank in, I couldn't help but wonder about the deeper mysteries surrounding the DAD. My mind raced with theories and speculations, but I had no concrete answers. One thing was for certain—Erin was on our side, so it seemed.

Zahra and I gathered around Erin as she beckoned us to come closer. Her eyes were filled with a mix of worry and excitement. It was clear that something big was about to happen.

"Listen carefully," Erin whispered, her voice barely audible over the crashing waves. "Atlantis is no longer safe here on Earth. We need to find a new home for my children."

My heart raced as I absorbed her words. Atlantis, the once hidden city, now faced an uncertain future. Erin suggested that Atlantis should join the DAD. It was capable of housing the entire city within itself. It was a daring plan, but one that held the promise of safety and salvation.

Cato contemplated Erin's proposal. After a moment of silence, he nodded solemnly, understanding the gravity of the situation. Atlantis needed a new beginning, and joining the DAD seemed like the best option. At first Cato wanted to stay and fight but Erin reminded him that even if the Atlanteans were willing to fight to a bitter end, Erin couldn't bear to watch this genocide take place. She would be driven to madness and prone to an evil far greater than her brother knowing her new chimeran body's potential. Cato, understanding his mother's reason, deferred to her better judgment. He ordered all surviving Atlanteans to prepare for an island-wide transport.

As for Zahra, an unconscious Francis, and myself, we decided to leave the island, but not without keeping a safe distance. We climbed aboard a small boat, our hearts heavy with the weight of what we were leaving behind. Erin told us that Francis would wake up soon. The Zephyran's were planning to use Francis as a sleeper agent but she made sure the augments she did to

Francis 'mind will prevent further tampering.

Erin approached us one last time, gratitude etched across her face. "Thank you for fighting for our cause," she said, her voice tinged with emotion. "We will never forget what you have done for Atlantis."

Our minds were then augmented to always be able to see a Zephyran no matter where they were. This was Erin's thanks for everything we did for them. Cato could do the same but on a limited time scale. Erin revealed to us that Cato's psychokinetic power was a blueprint for what she would later create as a power set within Erica.

Suddenly, as if on cue, the island began to rumble beneath the waves. We watched in awe-struck silence as it slowly rose from the ocean. It was a breathtaking sight, mesmerizing and yet filled with an eerie sense of mystery.

"Farewell me mates!" Erin said to us as her figure dissipated.

Before our eyes, a giant portal materialized, its swirling energy casting an otherworldly glow. Without warning, the island surged forward into the portal, defying the laws of nature, and disappeared within seconds after going through. The portal closed behind it, leaving nothing but a haunting silence in its wake.

We returned to Rayloria only to find our own set of troubles. What happened in Area 51 reached Zyra's notice.

Chapter 14

I never thought I would see the day when my detective skills would land me in a courtroom, accused of treason. But here I stood, alongside Zahra and Francis, in the heart of Zyra's justice system.

The Zyran Police took us into custody the moment we stepped off the Sector A's space shuttle. In court, We accused of collaborating with the Atlanteans in infiltrating and shutting down Area 51. The charge was serious—treason. We were being accused of betraying our country, our allegiance, and everything we stood for as TTA detectives.

As the trial began, I could feel the weight of uncertainty pressing against me. The evidence presented against us seemed overwhelming, leaving little room for doubt. But deep down, I couldn't accept that we were being framed. There had to be something more to this twisted plot.

Just as we were losing hope, a glimmer of opportunity emerged. Zyra, in a surprising turn of events, offered us a chance to clear our names. She gave us permission to find the truth, to uncover evidence that could prove our innocence. The court was adjourned and we were given a 1 week to prove that we weren't traitors and that these charges were false.

Feeling a surge of determination, we started our investigation. But things took a peculiar turn when Val appeared out of nowhere. She claimed to have vital information that could lead us to the real culprit—Ivon. As happy as I was to see her, I knew her presence meant something ominous was on the horizon. This time, I knew that Ivon planned to have us eliminated just to cover his hide. Val told me that the Ivon were looking for is hiding in her dimension.

Which begs the question. Is she a native to Chris' dimension? If so, what really happened and why was she really exiled? I had my own answer but Val played it off, making me think I was wrong. What we soon realized was that what I believed wasn't far off from what really happened.

When we entered Chris' timeline, we found ourselves in a run down hospital in Sector D. The sick and disabled surrounded us. The plight of those continuously oppressed by the Queen was a sight that sickened me. The once great General Mellis and his dream was dashed to pieces by a traitor in his midst. Our General knew the risks and Sigma was the one who tried to do something about it with the invention of time travel.

"I should've never created it." we heard a remorseful voice in one of the rooms. When we looked, we saw a tattered woman in a straight jacket.

Val told us that the war made Sigma go crazy. Losing the General and most of her family broke her. Only Sigma and Zyra were the last remaining family members of the Mellis family left alive. Sigma, in her minds eye believed she was

alone even though Zyra was still.
Zyra was grieving in her own way.
She kept busy with helping the
survivors in Sector D continue
fighting while her cousin was just
only a fragment of herself.

Val tried using her powers to heal
Sigma's pain but she failed, seeing
that her pain wasn't mental, but
emotional if not something deeper.
Val admitted she couldn't heal
trauma of the soul. The latter is what
Sigma felt, believing this broken
reality was her fault. The famous
Time Guru now brought to madness
by the fruits of her own invention.
Zahra was saddened; doubting at
first that such a dark timeline even
existed. Yet Val believed we weren't
without hope.

Despite how bleak this timeline was,
those who still believed in the
General's dream looked up to Val,
like she was some kind of savior.
The orphans, many who became
such from losing their parents to all
the fighting, saw Val as their mother.
To her, Val felt caring for them gave
her purpose in life ever since she left

TTA. UMOTE knows they can't beat her one on one but believes destroying her world proved more effective—that being those whom she swore to protect.

With determination, Val envisioned a day were the Hill-Adegas, along with UMOTE, ceased to exist in her reality and the people would take back their world from the evils within it. This was the hope Val lived by and by that same hope, she believed would break Sigma from her deep despair. She was the last of the Mellis Family and Val was going to make sure UMOTE could never reach her. The four of us prepared to march on Holy Manor but this time, things were far different.

When we reached the place, it was far more heavily guarded with AI, instead of cult followers. Yet these AI were built to be stealthy, perhaps made for assassination and not frontline assault. Val noted this as we fought our way to the heart of Holy Manor.

As we entered the inner courtyards of the heavily fortified Holy Manor, my heart raced with anticipation. That's when 2ndMillenium, Othniel Chris Goodman, confronted us. With him were a half dozen Ninjabots. As I approached him, I couldn't help but notice the anger etched on his face.

"I kinda figured one of my goody-two-shoes doppelgangers was helping this TTA reject!" He yelled in contempt.

He was not pleased about our unexpected arrival, to say the least. But resolving conflicts was what I did best, and I was determined to get to the bottom of this chaos.

"What made you turn?" I asked him.

"UMOTE," His voice broke into a tone of extreme sadness as he explained his Zahra's fate, "brutally murdered her."

That's when I shortly reflected on my relationship with my Zahra. Would I have quickly turned my back on a country I swore to protect?

It was a thought worth considering but I believed the answer was an emphatic hecky no!

Loosing a loved one is no excuse to turning evil. Francis, and his love for pop culture had to bring up a certain Jedi turned Sith Lord to correlate the deplorable transformation Chris underwent. It was inexcusable. I had no sympathy for him. Neither did the rest of my team. My Zahra though, stood quiet for a while until Chris stopped drowning in his own misery. Yet he wouldn't until she cursed at him, telling him to shut up.

"She wouldn't have wanted this!" Zahra reasoned.

"How would you know?" He retorted. "You're nothing like my Zahra!"

The manner of disrespect was enough. I started to feel a burning sensation, one echoing Val's sentiments against the evil within this twisted timeline. The cycle had to end. TTA in this world was far more sinister. Silas and his team knew not of the evil crap of a world they first entered. If they believed aiding Chris and his TTA back then did anything towards tipping the scales in favor of true justice, it was in vain. My TTA weren't going to make the same mistake.

In this twisted timeline, Chris explained how he took on a sinister role after his Zahra's death, betraying the Mellis' trust by eliminating the entire family with his UMOTE resources. Val was his subordinate yet she went rogue after learning of what he was doing and ran. Lord Emmanuel had her branded as public enemy number one and UMOTE hunted her in every timeline. They knew how to find her signature throughout the multiverse because she used TTA tech to traverse it. She was being tracked. Val, however, because of her powers, knew when they arrived and ran to another reality when she sensed their presence.

As I pieced together the puzzle, a sense of determination washed over me. I knew that I had to bring justice to this world's Zahra's memory and stop Lord Emmanuel's plans from unfolding. The weight of the world rested on our shoulders, but I was willing to bear the burden alone. Chris and his TTA couldn't continue operating as they were.

As I stood face to face with Chris, the tension crackled in the air like electricity. The rogue TTA agents fought tooth and nail against Zahra, Francis, and Val, but Chris had something else up his sleeve. Waves of nimble ninjabots surged forward, their metallic frames glinting in the dimly lit room. Just as Chris seemed to gain an upper hand, reinforcements arrived. However, these were no ordinary soldiers. They were heavier armored AI, designed to strike fear into the hearts of even the bravest warriors.

But I knew that Val possessed an incredible power, an awesome display of electrokinetic supremacy that could obliterate anything in her path. With a swift motion of her hand, Val unleashed a surge of thunderous energy, obliterating the

AI and reducing the mobile suits, once powered by humans, to mere scraps of bloody infused metal. The room echoed with the sound of destruction as the battle raged on.

Some specialized bots had forcefields but these protective shields buckled under the sheer power of the attacker. The end result was a much messier ending for the AI and human pilots alike.

It became clear that Chris had a plan as he disappeared into the chaotic battlefield. I ran after him but unaware of the deadly trap I would walk into. He lured me into a trap, hoping to catch me off-guard. But what he didn't know was that my quantum chain held a secret power, an innate ability to help me dodge near-fatal attacks. Time seemed to slow down, giving me the split-second advantage I needed to evade any attack that could end my life.

I could see the frustration building on Chris' face as his attacks missed their mark, time and time again. It was then that I noticed something peculiar. His quantum chain, the very source of his power, was defective. It flickered and sputtered, causing his movements to be erratic and unpredictable. The more he used its nanotech powers to defend himself against my attacks, the more he was punished for using them. Ever shock he felt from the chain around his neck knocked him off balance. As the battle raged on, it became a game of cat and mouse. Chris, desperate to overcome his malfunctioning chain, launched attack after attack, but each time I effortlessly dodged his blows—he was becoming more and more sloppy in his form.

We circled each other, locked in a deadly dance, as the room around us crumbled under the weight of our power. With every dodge, Chris grew more frustrated, his attacks becoming wild and reckless. I could see the doubt creeping into his eyes, his confidence waning with each passing moment. And then, in a moment of vulnerability, I seized my opportunity. I struck with precision and force, my quantum chain guiding me with unparalleled accuracy.

Chris stumbled backward, unable to defend himself against my onslaught. His weakened quantum chain could no longer protect him from my calculated strikes. As our battle came to an end, Chris lay defeated at my feet. The room fell silent, save for our heavy breaths and the distant echoes of our clash.

The rest of my team met up with me. All of them looked down on Chris' battered and bloody body. I glanced back at my team, believing I had won the battle after seeing Chris was unable to continue the fight.

"Good, you can all die together!" Chris cackled evilly.

I quickly looked at him and saw his body beginning to slowly pulse a white color.

"Oh no you don't!" Val warned.

Suddenly, a blue forcefield enveloped Chris and he was lifted in the air.

"How much pressure can your little forcefield take?' He mocked Val. "I doubt it can contain this blast. Nor are you fast enough to send me out the nearest airlock. You weren't fast enough to save your parents or the Mellis family and you won't be fast enough to save those around you."

"Enough!" Val screamed at him. In a flash of red light, the sphere containing Chris faded from existence.

"Where did you send them?" Zahra asked.

Suddenly, the sound of screams coming from inside Holy Manor erupted. Val formed a wall of energy before us, protecting all those outside the compound from what was to come—a gigantic explosion. Those human guards who ran for their lives after seeing Chris appear before them were beating on the energy wall, trying to breakthrough. They begged Val to let them out. Their last moments were in extreme horror as they looked into the eyes of their apathetic killer. The force of the blast destroyed everything not protected by Val's field. When the dust settled, Holy Manor was no more. What was in its place was tons of molten metal.

Those Raylorians who witness this awe-inspiring turn of events rejoiced. To us, it was yet another reality free of the tyrannical Hill-Adega regime. Val believed the war wasn't over yet because her parent's murderer was still out there. Chris wasn't the one who pulled the trigger. We surmised that she was talking about Ivon. But which one?

Then Lord Emmanuel appeared in the midst of the rubble of Holy Manor. He seemingly taunted Val, beckoning to follow him. We chased after Val as she went after him and through a portal.

Chapter 15

The sun bore down on us mercilessly as we stepped onto the barren soil of Mars. It seemed like a dream, or perhaps a nightmare, but there was no denying the reality of our situation. Zahra, Francis and I had chased Ivon through a portal behind Val, only to find ourselves in a world controlled by the Zephyran. As we surveyed our surroundings, it became clear that this was no desolate wasteland. The famous red planet known as Mars had been terraformed. Its atmosphere now resembled that of Earth. The air was thin, but breathable. It was a strange sight, to say the least. Remembering that this was not our Mars helped me focus on the mission before us.

The Zephyran had truly made the Martian frontier their home planet. Yet they were a malevolent force that needed to be stopped. Val wanted to put an end to Lord Emmanuel's reign but the Zephyran was standing in her way. We were going to clear that path for her. We moved cautiously throughout the capitol city known as Phyl Prime, hiding from the Zephyran patrols that roamed the landscape. Our objective was clear: find Ivon, but we needed Val as our guide in order to do that. She was nowhere to be found when we emerged on the other side of the portal.

We had almost lost hope when Val finally did appear and seemingly out of thin air. She explained that she had lost Ivon in the midst of a fight. He used his own Zephyran soldiers as a distraction to escape. She was certain that he was hiding in the Capitol building known as the Tower of Oak, deep within a forest. It was located in the center of the city.

Val told us that this forest was unlike anything I had ever seen. Towering trees reached towards the sky, their branches intertwined in a mesmerizing dance. But it was not just the beauty of the place that struck me; it was the sense of foreboding that hung in the air. The Tower of Oak was heavily fortified, surrounded by a giant thorn wall that seemed impenetrable. To get near the Tower, we had to use a secret tunnel that Zephyran insurgents built to mount an attack against Lord Ivon and his regime. I found it hard to believe that any Zephyran would be disloyal to anyone on Eric's side. Then again, whose to say all of his children are just as human as him and can see through his sham of a rule? As we approached the forest, tension grew within our group. We knew the risks involved, but there was no turning back now.

As the cold wind rustled through the leaves of the forest leading surrounding the Tower of Oak, I found myself standing before an intriguing sight. Yet we found that the forest's labyrinth was created to keep enemies of Lord Emmanuel from ever getting to his domain. However, opposition to his regime revealed to us revealed earlier that the existence of an underground tunnel that led straight to the maze's exit.

Determined to uncover the secrets hidden within, I found myself embarking on this daring adventure. Alongside Zahra and Francis, we followed Val as she led the way into the depths of the tunnel. The tunnel's darkness enveloped us, amplifying the tension that lingered in the air.

Emerging from the tunnel's mouth, we were abruptly met by the formidable Capitol guards of the Zephyran. Panic began to seize us as they encircled our small group. How could they have known we would use this hidden passage? Our secret was exposed. But how? They then told us that one of the rebels they captured told them the tunnel's location. Okay, not really surprising. How can you hide your thoughts from a telepath when you're one yourself? I highly doubt that rebel willingly gave up that info. The Zephyran have been known to be very deceitful in their tactics against their enemies.

We were quick to dispose of the guards before continuing towards our destination but we faced another roadblock—more guards rather. Val's power shielded us from the

Zephyran guards' detection. However, Val warned us that a strong enough Zephyran mind could detect us.

Pressing on, our determination drowning out the sound of the forest. Suddenly, the tranquil silence was shattered as a lone Zephyran guard emerged from the tower on patrol. His piercing gaze scanned the surroundings, and I could feel his mind reaching out, searching for any abnormality. This Zephyran seemingly had a strong mind. Val had trouble keeping us hidden from his detection.

Before anyone could react, the guard's eyes locked onto us, his telepathic senses picking up on our hidden presence. Without warning, he fired telekinetic blasts at us. With lightning speed, the battle commenced.

The night was thick with tension as we stood on the edge of the battle-ravaged forest. Val grew increasingly frustrated with our constant retreats whenever the

Zephyran reinforcements arrived. I could see the determination in her eyes, a fierce gleam that promised both danger and desperation. Without uttering a word, Val raised her hands to the heavens and dropped them. Just as quickly as she did, a bolt of lightning knocked waves of Zephyran guards off their feet.

"You can all burn!" Val cackled evilly as she dropped several more lightning bolts from heaven in quick succession. Suddenly, a stray bolt hit a tree near by and it caught on fire. Before long, the fire started spreading.

As flames danced on the tip, I watched, conflicted by the moral implications of her actions. But there was no time for hesitation. Val added fuel to the fire by lighting up other trees with her lightning strikes. Soon thereafter, the bush wall protecting the Tower of Oak was ablaze. The chaos erupted before us as the fire spread rapidly, creating a mesmerizing spectacle. The Zephyran soldiers were immediately drawn to the commotion, their frantic attempts to extinguish the flames only aided our diversion. Seizing the opportunity, Zahra, Francis, Val, and I slipped through the chaos and darted towards the towering walls of the Capitol.

As we raced through the corridors of the Tower of Oak, I couldn't help but feel a sense of thrill mixed with trepidation. The air was heavy with the scent of smoke, and the sound of crackling flames echoed through the halls. We knew the risks we were taking were immense, as even the Zephyran soldiers who ventured too close to the inferno were engulfed in frightening pyres.

With every step we took, we encountered higher-level Zephyrans, each one more formidable than the last. Our hearts pounded in our chests as we engaged in heated battles, our will to survive echoing in each swing of our weapons. The strength of our camaraderie and our shared purpose propelled us forward, despite the overwhelming odds.

Finally, after what felt like an eternity, we reached the top floor of the Tower of Oak.

In the center of the room was Lord Emmanuel, surrounded by a few high ranking Zephyran. He wore a smug smile as he congratulated us. Ivon's voice dripped with malice as he warned us that we wouldn't be leaving this place alive. His words hung heavily in the air, filling the room with tension. We exchanged glances, a mixture of determination and fear reflected in our eyes.

Without hesitation, the battle erupted. Swords clashed, sparks flew, and the air crackled with energy. Ivon's bodyguards fought fiercely, their skills matched only by their loyalty. But one by one, they fell, their lives snuffed out by our unwavering determination. Val, with her extraordinary powers, stepped forward. She mustered every ounce of her strength and unleashed a devastating attack.

"You're not going anywhere!" Val yelled at Ivon. In an instant, a brilliant explosion of light consumed Ivon. He was vaporized into nothingness. His sinister presence vanished, leaving behind an eerie silence.

As the dust settled, Val's eyes gleamed with victory. She had done it. She had stopped Ivon in his tracks. The fight he had with her was quicker than we all realized even though we were fixated on defeating his guards. She told us that she manipulated time itself to counteract his quantum chain's ability to dodge fatal attacks.

"He always used it to get away from me at the last second." Val explained.

The impossible had become possible. After years of trying to avenge her family's death, Val's mission was complete. She had us to thank for that.

We learned we couldn't stay in the tower any longer as the ground shook beneath us. Val saw with her mind's eye that the fires below had consumed every Zephyran in the surrounding areas of the Tower. The fire continued to spread wildly into the forest maze. The tower started to collapse but before it did, we followed Val through a portal back to the hospital on Rayloria.

Chapter 16

The air in the hospital room was thick with a tangible sense of anticipation. Val, Zahra, Francis, and I stood before Sigma. Sigma, in her catatonic state, was still trapped in a straight jacket, her vacant eyes staring into nothingness.

Val touched Sigma's forehead with two gentle fingers before closing her eyes. Tears streamed down Val's face, a mixture of sadness and relief. She had seen what had become of our friend and it was heartbreaking. But in that moment, something changed. Val's tears transformed, as if by some mystical force, into tears of joy.

Sigma slowly leaned forward, as if struggling against the restraints of her straight jacket. Her voice, weak and trembling, stuttered as she finally uttered her real name, Michelle Evanston. We couldn't believe what we were witnessing. Sigma, our dear friend who had been lost to us, was slowly emerging from her catatonic state.

With a renewed sense of hope, Sigma spoke, her words laced with urgency. "You need to stop running," she said, her voice barely a whisper. We exchanged puzzled glances, wondering what she meant. We had been on the run for so long, hiding from the dangers of the war that had consumed our lives.

Val, wiping away her tears, nodded solemnly. "I won't run anymore," she promised, her voice filled with determination. "The war's finally over."

As Val's words hung in the air, a silence filled the room, broken only by the distant hum of hospital machinery. We stood there, still processing the weight of Sigma's words and the revelation of her true identity. What had Sigma been running from all this time? And why did she choose this moment, in her fragile state, to tell us this?

That's when Val told us the rest of her story. Valencia Valentine was a pseudonym she used to hide her real identity in every reality she visited. Valentine was her late mother's maiden name. Her mother's full name was Rica Valencia Valentine. Val wanted to use her mother's name to spook UMOTE every time they heard that name, like a boogyman/ghost. At first, Val's fear factor as low until she met Erin. In her own universe, the Lunninghams didn't exist and nor did their children. However, they exist in other parts of her universe because of the Lunninghams in ours.

Erin augmented Val's body with what she lady could now do, seeing her mission to stop UMOTE as noble. Erin's reason for helping Val was based on her deep-seated hatred for the Hill-Adega family and all that belongs to her brother. UMOTE, to a certain extent, is an ally of Lunningham through Ivon and his doppelgangers. I couldn't help but realize that the Lunningham's influence ran deep through many realities and every other powerful entity was either for them or a third party. Still, it was UMOTE that made our lives miserable with these charges against us.

I stood before Val, feeling the weight of disappointment settle heavy on my shoulders. She had tried her best, I knew that, but it wasn't enough. The false charges against my team and I still loomed over us like a dark cloud, threatening to tear apart our livelihoods.

"Val, I appreciate everything you've done," I said, my voice laced with regret. "But without concrete evidence, we're still at the mercy of those who seek to tarnish our reputation."

Val lowered her gaze, her apology hanging in the air between us. "I'm sorry, Othniel. I truly believed I could prove your innocence, but the matter won't be an issue anymore."

"Explain?" I demanded. Her suddenly relaxed demeanor over this subject was a bit suspicious.

"Zyra will find what she's looking for on her own." Val answered. "And when she does, Mwongo won't be able to roam freely throughout Rayloria or anywhere on the Lunar plane for that matter because he will be on Rayloria's Most Wanted list."

But even as we vowed to bring Mwongo to justice, I couldn't help but feel weariness settle over me. Years of chasing criminals through time had taken its toll, both physically and emotionally. My body ached, and my mind longed for respite.

"Maybe it's time we take a leave of absence," I mused, my voice tinged with exhaustion. "We've dedicated our lives to the TTA, but it's taken so much from us. Maybe it's time we take care of ourselves."

Francis and Zahra, my loyal teammates, exchanged glances, their weary faces reflecting my own sentiments. They had fought alongside me, risking everything for the sake of justice. It was only fair that they have a chance to heal as well.

"You're right, Othniel," Francis said, his voice filled with resolve. "We need a break. Our bodies and minds can't take much more. It's time to focus on ourselves for a while."

A sense of relief washed over me as I realized that I was not alone in this decision. We had been through so much together, and now it was time to prioritize our own well-being. Speaking of just that, my mind quickly went to Val's parents and the Evanstons from our reality.

"My father and your Evanstons are safe in PowerLand." Val said cheerfully.

What exactly was PowerLand and how could we get there? At the moment, we couldn't afford another detour.

"I just have a few more questions." I started. I needed to know more about Val for my own personal benefit.

"You must like spoilers, huh?" Val joked.

"Mildly." I retorted.

"Is the Val in our timeline friend or foe?". The questioned burned in my mind. If this unknown Val was anything like the one we've worked with, I would like to know who she was. A lingering thought whether or not she was valiant like this one or evil like Chris poked at my soul.

"Don't worry about her." Val assured. "She hasn't been born yet. Nor have her parents met."

"Then why use her family's history as your own?" Zahra sounded confused.

TTA once knew Val to be the daughter of Kayleen and Durk Daryl, as what Silas reported to his Doctor Chronos. Even down to who she was hunting was a stretched truth. Yet there really wasn't a difference between Mwongo and Wongo. Also, who's to say our Ivon took the title of Lord Emmanuel after learning of the untimely demise of his alternate reality doppelganger? Knowing the truth now, I still wondered where in the multiverse that particular Val was.

Though it seemed this Val used that family's history to hide her own for safety reasons, realistically, what she did could've jeopardized the existence of her alternate reality doppelganger. However, I believed she had contingencies in place to make sure that never happened. Then it dawned on me—GUB through UMOTE tried to assassinate her grandparents in our reality but TTA stopped the attempt. Clever lady!

"I don't anymore." Val sighed in relief. "By the time this Val is born in your world, no one will have remembered where I came from except you three, Zyra and Sigma."

"So you've met this other Val already?" I deducted.

"Of course!" Val laughed. "And she's also in TTA like we are!"

Interesting! Having Val with us piqued my curiosity—such a powerful being made possible by the ingenuity of Erin Lunningham. Ermm… Erica Lunningham. Alas, it was now time to let her and all those of this Rayloria rebuild their world. Clearing our names was of most importance now. So, we left back to our reality to face our justice system. I wanted to trust Val's word. Expecting the worse but the latter would soon be only in the recesses of my mind with what came next.

"Innocent of the Treason charge."
The jury unanimously decided.

The court roared in sighs and other sounds of relief. Zyra called us into her oval office to speak with us at length what she found. It was as Val suggested—someone who had ties to the GUB falsified the charges. There were several moles within her government that needed to be removed and after doing so, the charges against us were found to be only a ploy to remove a powerful piece off the board against our enemies.

Zyra began to speak, her voice filled with gratitude and intrigue. She revealed that she knew Val had something to do with the court deciding in our favor. Val, always one step ahead, had orchestrated a plan to help us escape the clutches of a kangaroo court, thus leading to a mistrial.

But Zyra's gratitude came with a somber realization. Val's top priority was to rebuild her own reality, a task that required all her attention and resources. While she had helped us, she couldn't afford to be caught up in our drama any longer. The best she did was point Zahra in the right direction with the resources she currently had.

As Zyra and Sigma thanked us for our bravery and dedication to justice, I couldn't help but feel a mix of emotions: Relief at our newfound freedom, gratitude for Val's assistance, and yet a lingering sense of unease. Why? I knew UMOTE and their allies would try again. Either against us personally or threaten Rayloria's utopic borders with their evil. None of us could ever let our guard down ever again.

The energy in the room shifted drastically as Zyra looked at me and said, "Othniel, I have a surprise for you." Before I could utter a word, she continued, "All of you can take a vacation from your official TTA duties. All of you deserve it."

My heart skipped a beat as the idea of a well-deserved break from the demanding world as a time-traveling detective. The weight of my responsibilities seemed to lift off my shoulders. I couldn't believe my luck, and a smile spread across my face.

"Oh, and by the way, Zahra is two months pregnant with your child." Zyra said coyly.

My eyes widened, and my mind raced to catch up with this unexpected revelation. It felt like the universe was showering us with blessings beyond our wildest dreams. I looked over to my love and she gave me an innocent look, folding her arms and biting her lip.

"I was gonna tell you sooner or later." Zahra said in a warm tone.

Zyra couldn't resist teasing us about the antiquated Nairan Code. Under its defunct laws, Zahra and I would have faced severe consequences for our relationship. But times had changed, and we were free to embrace this new chapter in our lives.

To commemorate the joyous occasion, Zyra suggested a makeshift wedding ceremony before we embarked on our vacation. Government officials, along with our fellow TTA agents Francis and Sigma, gathered as witnesses. It was an unconventional affair, but love knows no boundaries, and it was a moment of pure happiness.

With our vows exchanged and our love sealed in the presence of our loved ones and co-workers, Zahra and I embarked on our much-deserved vacation along with a

trusted companion, Francis. The days
were filled with laughter, love, and
anticipation for the new life growing
within Zahra's womb.

Epilogue

I never thought I would find myself in such a peculiar situation. The year is 2030, and my wife Zahra and I are eagerly awaiting the arrival of our daughter, Celes Lina Goodman. In anticipation of her birth, we decided to spend our honeymoon in Zahra's hometown of New Delhi. However, instead of staying in the bustling city, we made an unusual choice—we opted to have a villa built on the outskirts, deep in the countryside, away from civilization.

The idea was to have a serene and secluded place where our growing family could find peace and tranquility. It seemed like the perfect plan. Even Francis offered to accompany us. Being a detective myself, I couldn't refuse his assistance. Little did I know that our honeymoon would turn into a mysterious and intriguing adventure.

As we arrived at the construction site, I noticed something odd about the workers. They were not human, but AI Raylorian construction workers. These artificial beings were highly advanced, capable of constructing the most intricate designs with utmost precision. The villa we had envisioned was slowly taking shape, thanks to their tireless efforts.

The AI construction crew was a gift from Zyra for the duration of the project. Francis was the one who made it happen. He definitely had our thanks. Now the two of us had a home we could be proud of and raise our daughter together.

Within the next few months, our villa was completed. Suddenly, a woman approached our villa's gates. A woman, dressed in a cloak of deep purple, stood before me, her eyes gleaming with determination. Her face was hidden beneath it until she lowered it. Revealing a light skinned face with a vertical color split hair. The colors were half black and half red. However, what was the most interesting about her were the ears. They were pointed—as if she was an elf. Wait! They don't exist! Hmmm, maybe in her reality they do.

"Hello, Othniel," she said, her voice carrying a hint of familiarity.

"I'm sorry, do I know you?" I asked, puzzled by her presence.

"My name is Z'Rahna Kynnor," she replied, a hint of a smile tugging at her lips. "I used to work with your father, Josiah, many years ago."

My heart skipped a beat at the mention of my father's name. I had spent countless hours searching for any trace of him, but all my efforts had been in vain. "You--you knew my father?" I stammered, a mixture of excitement and disbelief swirling within me.

Z'Rahna nodded, her gaze intense. "I remember Josiah fondly," she said. "But my search for him ended long ago, shortly after our team was scattered throughout time."

Seeing the disbelief in my eyes, Z'Rahna continued. "You need to give up your search of him. He's lost to the Space-Time Continuum."

I suddenly felt a sense of hopelessness that my old man was somewhere out there, never to be found again. I still wanted to know, since Z'Rhana stopped looking for my dad, what has she been doing since then.

"I've been hunting Master Mwongo all these years," she explained. "He is a dangerous force, and the influence of his followers, mainly UMOTE and GUB through them."

"Is it true that the Zephyran are here on Earth, still?" Zahra asked. We both knew that what we did in Area 51 was only temporary. The Zephyran would put another stranglehold on it soon after they recovered from that loss.

"Yes." Z'Rhana answered nervously. "That's why we need to be on guard against them if they find us. I came here to make good on my vow to protect your family."

Her words resonated within me, igniting a fire of determination. I had spent my life solving mysteries and unraveling enigmas, and now, I had a new mission—to ensure that my family flourished. Z'Rhana seemed to be all in on making that journey a success.

I wanted to know more about Z'Rhana. Why the strange appearance? Was she not born a human?

"Erica Lunningham is to thank for my transformation." Z'Rhana explained.

I should've known Z'Rhana knew the good doctor. Only two humans have ever ventured beyond our solar system and if you happened to be a traveler of cosmos, you will run into either doctor or those associated with them. Fortunately for Z'Rhana, she met the more benevolent of the two.

"If it hadn't have been for her, I would've died from radiation poisoning." Z'Rhana explained. "Where I found myself after our team was scattered was in a place Erin happened to be with some plant moss race known as the Gridth.”

Good to know Erica is still the one to help others in need. I hope she stays like that. Then I began to tell Z'Rhana about Ivon and the threat he posed to our family but before I could utter a single word, she held up her hand, silencing me. A knowing smile played on her lips, betraying the depth of her knowledge.

“I already know about Ivon, Othniel,” she said, her voice cool and determined. “I know about the many evils he and his doppelgängers have committed.”

So there's no need for debriefing her. I took she didn't wanna hear our missions where he was always there to get in our way. Still, I believed justice wasn't done until Ivon and those who supported his ideals were rendered inert.

“He's untouchable,” Z'Rahna continued, her eyes narrowing with determination. “He's surrounded by

Eric's Zephyran. But I won't let him continue to wreak havoc on innocent lives. There has to be a way to stop him and also Eric Lunningham."

I could see Z'Rahna was on a personal mission, a mission to stop the Ivon at all costs. And she revealed two key figures in her plan—2kReturner and the Forest Flower. Here I thought Zahra and I would have a break from our time-traveling detective work. Embracing those two names was in our future and it should be now rather than later.

"Until the mission is ready to go, I offer to be Celes' godmother," Z'Rahna said, her voice softening. She raised her voice once more, determined as ever as she continued, "I will protect her with my life, just as I swear to one day end Ivon's influence over the multiverse. Then, Eric is next!"

I couldn't help but admire Z'Rahna's resolution, her unwavering resolve to bring justice to a world plagued by the Ivon's malevolence. And so we willingly accepted Z'Rhana into our daughter's life, knowing that she would be a guiding light in not just our daughter's darkest hours but the entire family's.

In the months to come, Z'Rahna became an integral part of Celes' life, a loving and protective presence that brought comfort and reassurance to the Goodman household. She was also the one who delivered our daughter. Francis stayed around too. Celes found his jokes amusing.

"Uncle Karr is so bizarre." A young Celes would often say to him in front of everyone. Her words would incite others to laugh. Francis was always the bizarre one—even to Celes. At least he kept her happy. Celes had your average toddler temper tantrums but Francis knew how to calm a raging child with his jokes and overall goofiness.

As for Z'Rhana, she held fast to being the protective aunt. We wouldn't have it any other way. Her powerset was similar to Val's, minus the electrokinesis. She too was a telepath—perhaps an even better one than Val herself!

Until the day of our next mission, this is farewell. For now, our family is my main focus.

Appendix
2kReturner
By Othello Gooden Jr.

They call him 2kReturner of Zyra
No matter where you are!
Someday he shall solve
All of Zyra's mysteries

They call him 2kReturner of Zyra
No matter where he be!
Just like it was last century
This is far from the end of his story!

Whether it's deep in the past
Fixing a temporal fissure
Caused by a villainous contender
Or far into an alternate future
Where there's a societal rupture

Know one thing…
Whatever the case…
This is his nebula!

About the Author

Othello Gooden Jr. was born on January 13, 1985 in Cincinnati, Ohio. At an early age he learned the basics of reading, speaking, and writing while attending ministry school. Throughout his school years till now, he expressed those abilities in multiple online communities. Upon graduating from the School for Creative and Performing Arts in 2004, majoring in instrumental music, Othello enrolled in University of Cincinnati Raymond Walters College's Computer Support Technology program. While there, he learned the basics of MS Office, Object Programming, journalism, and animation. His passion for writing continued as Othello entertained his peers and teachers with his stories.

After graduating in 2009, Othello started creating videos on YouTube, first beginning with 2kReturner